Monica

Delaney Diamond

Garden Avenue Press

Monica by Delaney Diamond

Copyright © 2022, Delaney Diamond

Garden Avenue Press

Atlanta, Georgia

ISBN: 978-1-946302-67-0 (Ebook edition)

ISBN: 978-1-946302-68-7 (Paperback edition)

www.delaneydiamond.com

Chapter One

"Wake up."

Monica moaned and pulled the weighted blanket over her head, burrowing deeper in the bed as if ignoring her assistant's voice would make Daisy go away.

Why couldn't the day start at noon? With a morning meeting on her calendar, staying out all night had not been the best decision. Cranky and tired, all she wanted to do was stay in bed.

"You need to get ready before it's too late," Daisy said.

Monica heard her puttering around the room, but with a sleep mask over her eyes and the linens pulled over her head, she remained in a dark cocoon.

"Come on, Monica." Daisy shook her by the shoulders.

"Go away," Monica mumbled into the pillow.

"I can't. You'll fire me if I do."

Her assistant yanked the blanket off her body, and Monica released an exaggerated sigh.

"I hate you."

"I know," Daisy said, unperturbed.

Monica shoved the black satin mask off her eyes and sat up against the tufted headboard and half a dozen pillows, squinting into the glare coming through the opened blackout drapes. Swinging her legs off the bed, she stared groggy-eyed at the tray of food Daisy had placed on the table, mouth watering at the sight of her requested meal of a soft-boiled egg, bacon, and toast.

Daisy came to stand in front of her, hands on her hips. Almost as tall as Monica, with the same russet-brown complexion, she wore her hair in a layered bob. Monica had shaved off her hair months ago, cutting it so low she couldn't do a simple plait if she wanted to.

"Are you awake?" Daisy asked in an amused tone.

"Barely."

Daisy handed over her cell phone, and Monica pushed up from the mattress. Eyes glued to the screen, she checked activity on Instagram and Twitter, padding around the cushiony two-person loveseat at the foot of the bed.

She hadn't missed much overnight, so she fired off a quick *Good morning, bitches!* tweet and headed into the bathroom.

"I guess you had fun last night?" Daisy called.

"I did," Monica called back, a smile touching her lips, thinking about all the wild partying from the night before.

She had met Dante, an aspiring actor, at a gala event when she took a short trip to LA to visit her stepbrother. On his way to Florida, Dante stopped in Atlanta to see her.

"The man is foine," Daisy remarked.

"He is fine," Monica agreed.

"No, he's *foine*," Daisy corrected.

"You're right," Monica chuckled.

Women constantly eye-balled him because of his good looks and fine physique. Not that it mattered. She didn't want to marry the guy. They were having fun, and she long ago decided marriage and commitment were not in the cards for her.

Stripping out of her ivory colored pajamas short set, she stepped into the shower stall. Warm water poured over her head and face and trickled down her body, and she moaned and smiled into the spray as she woke up, slowly starting to feel like herself.

After her shower, she brushed her teeth and washed her face with a new skincare line she was testing out for a potential endorsement deal, and then strolled into the bedroom in a fluffy white robe monogrammed with her initials over the left breast.

Her room was decorated in ivory silks, gold, and Earth tones with custom upholstery and drapery, and the bed's tufted headboard and canopy added to the luxurious decor. When her mother okayed the redecoration of her room a year ago, Monica added a gold leaf pattern to the ceiling's center dome to highlight the crystal chandelier above the bed. She also had the contractor install a platform in the alcove in front of the windows, where two chairs sat across a small table from each other.

Stepping onto the platform, she sank into a chair and began eating her meal. Daisy poured warm tea into a white teacup and drizzled in honey before handing it to Monica.

"Thank you," she murmured, taking a sip.

Today was a big day. She seemed calm on the outside, but inside, she was ecstatic. As a social media influencer, she often partnered with brands on sponsorship deals, but today's contract would be her most lucrative yet.

For the past few years she had accumulated a huge number of followers on her social media accounts on Twitter and Instagram. She started small, showing off her day-to-day as a young woman living an enviable life, which included images of her partying, wearing the latest haute couture, and posing on yachts while vacationing around the world.

Advertisers took notice of the high engagement on her Instagram account. Her famous-for-doing-nothing persona confused her family, particularly her brother Ethan, who didn't view social media influencer as a real job. But she managed a small staff of contractors, which included her assistant, Daisy. Coupled with her personal investments, she earned a comfortable living.

Business was so good she didn't need to solicit deals. Brands came to her. Though they paid her to endorse products, she never promoted anything she didn't believe in or use herself. It hadn't been easy to stick to her principles, especially with the amount of money some companies threw at her, but if nothing else, she had her integrity and didn't want to betray the trust of her fans.

As she sipped the tea, Daisy exited her closet with two outfits. Holding one in each hand on a hanger, she asked, "You wanted to see the red and ivory suits?"

Chewing a piece of toast, Monica nodded. "I can't decide. I need to try them both," she said.

"Okay." Daisy gently placed the outfits on the bed and disappeared into the walk-in closet.

While her assistant brought out shoes, tops, underwear, and accessories, Monica hurried through breakfast. When she finished, she dusted off her hands and picked up the white suit.

"I'll try this one first."

She slipped on her underwear and then donned the outfit. Checking out her appearance in the full-length mirror, she turned left and then right, switching out accessories and jewelry for different effects. They both agreed she rocked all the combinations, but she wasn't completely satisfied.

4

Then she tried the red suit and mixed and matched accessories and jewelry with it. Finally, she rested her hands on her hips. "I like the red because it makes me look powerful," she said to Daisy, who stood behind her.

Her assistant nodded. "I know what you mean, but I think the red is too much."

"But the white suit isn't enough," Monica pointed out. She gasped. "I could wear both."

"What do you mean?"

"Wear red and white."

Daisy's eyes widened. "You're a genius! Combining the two would be perfect. White top or red top?"

"Red top," they said at the same time.

They laughed, and Monica took the white pants from her assistant's arm.

"Let's see how this looks," she said, shimmying out of the other slacks.

After she put on the red slacks, she started her twists and turns again, but this time no frown marred her forehead. The combination of the two colors worked very well together.

With a burst of inspiration, she removed her silk top and bra but kept the jacket buttoned to the middle of her torso. The deep vee neckline exposed an expanse of brown skin, which she could pull off with her small breasts. When she added huge gold hoop earrings and multi-colored sling backs, the outfit was complete.

"Perfect," Daisy said with genuine admiration. "You're going to knock 'em dead."

"Darn right." Monica rested her hands on her hips and grinned into the mirror.

Nigel Chambers had reached out to her agent a while back and made the offer. Today, they were getting together with the lawyers to sign the paperwork. Normally she did everything virtually, but he'd insisted he wanted to meet in person before they signed the contracts.

"I'm ready," she said, spinning away from the mirror.

Daisy checked her watch. "The car service should be here in exactly three minutes."

"I better get going then. You were able to get Marlon?" Monica double-checked her make up.

She had her own cars—a yellow Ferrari and a more subtle white Porsche Cayenne—but they were getting detailed.

"Of course. I know how to do my job, Monica," Daisy teased.

Monica laughed. "I know you do. I don't know what I'd do without you."

Daisy had worked with her for over six months, a referral from her attorney. Her last assistant had gotten married. Monica was happy for her, but losing such a great helper after two years bummed her out, the drawback to having someone constantly at her side. Her assistant met a lot of the same people, and the last one met a famous actor and they hit it off. Six months later, she needed a new assistant.

Considering she didn't have prior experience working as a personal assistant, Daisy did a wonderful job, paying such close to attention, at times she anticipated Monica's needs before *she* knew what she needed.

They exited the bedroom, her palm dragging along the wrought-iron handrail as she descended the bifurcated staircase into the opulent foyer.

"Sure you don't need me to come?" Daisy asked.

"No, I've got it," Monica said, head bent over her phone. Her tweet had already racked up thousands of likes, retweets, and responses. "Could you go through my IG DM's and check for offers? Someone tagged me on Twitter and said they sent a proposal, but I don't know what they're talking about. I haven't checked my DMs in weeks. I don't know why people don't follow the instructions on my profile." They were supposed to send proposals to her email, which Daisy sorted through for her.

"No problem," Daisy said. "I'll do that after I pick out the clothes for you to donate to the auction."

"Oh gosh, I forgot about the auction. When are they coming to pick up the items?"

"Tomorrow at noon."

"Good. I'll go through everything later this evening. Tahtah." She waved on her way out.

Marlon stood beside the car with the door open.

"Hey, Marlon."

"Hey, Miss Connor."

She rolled her eyes. "You and this "Miss Connor" business. I told you to call me Monica."

He laughed, shaking his head as she slid into the backseat. "And I told you first names are too familiar. Not my style."

When he sat in the driver seat she let out a loud sigh to convey her displeasure with his refusal to call her by her first name.

"All right. Get me safely to my destination, please."

He smiled at her in the rearview mirror. "Will do."

Chapter Two

"You working this weekend? The crew is thinking about playing baseball on Saturday. Same teams as last year."

Phone cradled between his shoulder and ear, Andre Campos sat with his feet crossed atop his desk, in an office on the third floor of a converted factory in Atlanta.

"I don't have time, man," he replied to his cousin, Phineas, who preferred to go by Phin because he hated his 'old man name.'

"You never have time to hang out. You always working."

Andre chuckled as he reviewed a printout of last week's liquor sales at Dynamic Lounge, one of multiple dining establishments Chambers Enterprises owned throughout the southeast.

"All you want to do is play or party all the time."

"You only thirty-one and sound like an old man already," his cousin accused.

"Because I want more out of life than seeing how many shots I can drink before I pass out?"

"You know it ain't like that."

"It's exactly like that. The baseball game is an excuse to go to a bar afterward and get drunk."

"You used to be fun. Now you all serious and shit."

"Because I'm *working*. You should try that one day."

That was an unfair statement. His cousin used to work as an accountant, but after a massive layoff at his company, he became unemployed.

"I'm on an extended vacation."

"When your severance money runs out, you'll be scrambling for a job and wish you'd put something away for a rainy day."

"Yeah, you old, bruh. That's something Grandpa Cy would say."

"And he'd be right. Listen, I gotta go. Some of us gotta work."

"Yeah, yeah. You just trying to impress that bougie chick and her daddy. I don't know why you like high maintenance women."

"Like you don't. Chelle ain't high maintenance?"

"A little bit, but she's worth it," he mumbled.

"Uh-huh. Look at your ass. She got a ring in your nose. Pathetic."

"Fuck you, man."

Andre let out a hearty chuckle. "Listen, I can't do Saturday, but how about you and me do brunch on Sunday?"

"Brunch. Like we girlfriends. A'ight, fine, if that's the only way I can get you to hang out, brunch it is. Wear a pretty dress."

"Fuck *you*."

Phin laughed as he hung up.

Andre dropped his feet to the floor and studied the figures on the printed sheet again. Dynamic Lounge had seen record

9

liquor sales over the weekend. The phone on his desk rang, and a quick glance indicated the caller was the managing partner, Nigel Chambers.

"Hello, Nigel."

"Andre! Glad I caught you at your desk. I need a favor." He sounded like he was in the car.

"Sure, no problem. What do you need?" Andre asked absentmindedly, flipping to the next sheet.

"I have an appointment to sign a contract with a social media influencer this morning, but I can't make the meeting. Belinda and I are on our way to look at a property for her store."

Belinda was his daughter, and three months ago Andre asked her to marry him. He often teased his fiancée about her ridiculous obsession with shoes. She had an entire closet solely for her shoes, filled with hundreds of pairs, many of which she had never worn. She clearly didn't need so many. To satisfy her desire to own and run a business, her father agreed to finance a boutique for her, and over the past few weeks they'd gone to see several properties, none of which satisfied the burgeoning entrepreneur.

"Which project is this for?" Andre asked.

"The new one at the 17th Street Hotel, Midnight Lounge."

Chambers Enterprises provided entertainment for older professionals and entrepreneurs across the southeast. However, this new project targeted a younger demographic, thanks to a suggestion from Andre.

"When's the meeting?" Andre asked.

"In five minutes."

Andre stifled a sigh. *Goddammit.*

"Short notice, I know, but it couldn't be helped. I need you to sign on behalf of the company since J.L. is out of town. Stanley is on his way, if he isn't there already. He prepared a power of attorney for you to sign the contract. Ms. Jones will have everything for you."

Andre earned a small salary at the company, but the bulk of his income came from being a silent partner, and as such he remained behind the scenes. The arrangement worked well for him. He contributed capital and generated a steady income as a result—income he used to pay the exorbitant fees required for an attorney to work on appeals for his mother. So far he'd put money into three properties—Dynamic Lounge, an expansion to another restaurant, and the soon-to-open Midnight Lounge.

"No problem, I'll take care of it," he said, rising from his chair.

"Thanks. I won't be in the office today. After I check out this property, I'm flying to Miami for a meeting, but I'll be back by this evening. Why don't you join me and Belinda at the house for dinner around seven?"

"Not a problem. I'll be there."

"Good. Talk to you later."

Andre hung up. He straightened his vest and pulled his charcoal jacket from the coat rack. As he crossed the carpet, Ms. Jones—Nigel's assistant—entered through the open door.

An older woman with medium-brown skin and mostly gray hair, her solemn, tart-looking face and pinched mouth reminded him of a school marm. Though she'd never said an rude word to him, he knew she hadn't liked when Nigel brought him on as an investor. Her critical eyes had assessed the rings on his fingers and tattoos on his forearms, and he was pretty sure she knew all about his past run-ins with the law as a juvenile.

"Mr. Chambers called. He wants you to take his place in a meeting downstairs," she said.

"I just got off the phone with him."

Ms. Jones handed over a pen and a sheet of paper. "Stanley

needs you to sign this POA. It's good for today and this contract only."

Andre scanned the document. Placing the sheet against the wall, he signed his signature as a legal representative for Nigel.

Ms. Jones took the page and pen and then handed over a folder. "Here is the final contract. Two copies. Stanley, Miss Connor, and her attorney are waiting for you."

His heart skipped a beat. "Miss Connor?"

Connor was not an unusual name, yet every time he'd heard it over the years, his body reacted the same. He tensed and became more alert.

"Yes, Miss Connor and her attorney are here. They're all in the small conference room downstairs." She stalked off.

Recovering quickly, Andre skimmed the contents of the folder as he walked the middle aisle of staff in their cubicles toward the elevator.

"Hey, Andre."

Several female employees greeted him, and he nodded and smiled, returning a friendly but distracted greeting.

The contract was between Connor Media, LLC and Chambers Enterprises. Connor Media would post several times up until and during the opening night of Midnight Lounge.

His eyebrows raised when he saw the cost per post.

"I'm in the wrong business," he muttered.

Advertising in today's world had changed. Influencers commanded hefty fees to promote products on their pages, so he wasn't surprised Nigel had gone this route, particularly since this project targeted young Black professionals with disposable income looking for like-minded people to network with and engage with socially.

He exited the elevator. Nigel chose to maintain the character of the building on the main floor, so exposed brick walls and high ceilings greeted visitors. To the left of the double doors, one male and one female receptionist stood behind a half-moon-shaped desk. They alternated between answering the phones and completing tasks for junior staff members.

Andre waved as he strolled toward the conference room. His eyes dipped back to the contracts in hand, and the name on the last page forced him to stop abruptly.

Clear as day, in black and white, he saw a name he hadn't seen in years.

Monica Connor. A dart of shock arrowed through him. Surely it couldn't be the same Monica Connor.

The conference room's closed mini-blinds kept him from seeing inside the conference room, but as he neared the door, his ab muscles tightened at the thought of seeing her. He hadn't seen her in... how long had it been? Nine years.

Nearing the door, he straightened his shoulders and double-checked his clothing was neat. He straightened his tie, glancing down at the pale green shirt, dark slacks, and shiny black shoes. He looked presentable. Not that he cared what she thought. She was someone from his past, and this was simply business.

Besides, the person in the conference room could be a different Monica Connor.

No such luck.

His breathing temporarily halted. He recognized her right away, despite cutting off all her hair and leaving a short buzz cut. He'd know those pretty chestnut eyes and high cheekbones anywhere. Large hoops almost touching her shoulders adorned her ears, but smaller earrings also climbed up the shell of her right ear.

She stood at one end of the long wood table, chatting with Stanley the company's attorney, and another woman, whom he assumed was her attorney. Her face glowed with health and vitality, hands animated as she talked. Red lipstick brightened her full lips and popped against her russet-brown skin.

She wasn't born into money but wore it well. Tall with slender curves poured into a red and white pants suit, he wasn't surprised she'd become an influencer. Monica Connor was the epitome of an "it" girl. Popular, with an engaging personality, she'd been a trendsetter back in college. He used to call her Sunshine because she had a glow about her and brightened his day with her appearance.

His gaze dipped to the skin revealed by the plunging neckline of the red jacket she wore as a shirt.

No bra.

His mouth went dry, and he licked his lips to counteract the parched, desert-like sensation when he assessed the halfway open top.

Her gaze shifted and their eyes met across the glass table. The smile on her face faltered before disappearing altogether, while he experienced the strangest sensation—as if the walls were closing in. She stared at him, and lips he'd known well—once upon a time—parted in shock.

"Andre." She whispered his name, and his scalp tingled under the sound of her voice. She flashed a brief grin, hands going to her hips. "It's good to see you."

Liar. The way-too-high octave of her voice indicated fake excitement.

He didn't smile back, unable to truly engage in the scene because never in a fifty million years had he expected Monica Connor to be standing in the building where he worked.

"Since you two know each other, the only introductions that need to be made are between Ms. Charles and you, Andre," Stanley said, clueless to the pulse of energy surging through the room.

A portly, balding man, he gave off the impression of an affable, grandfatherly type. In reality, he had teeth as sharp as a shark's when it came to contract negotiations. Nigel didn't sign anything without him reviewing it first.

"Penelope Charles, this is Andre Campos. He's taking the place of Mr. Chambers today because he was called away on a family emergency."

Andre handed over the folder.

"As long as his signature is binding, that's all I care about," Penelope said with a laugh.

Stanley smiled. "Absolutely. You have nothing to worry about."

Andre extended his hand and shook Penelope's. "Good to meet you."

"Likewise. Let's get this done, shall we?"

They all sat down, and Monica and her attorney flipped through the pages to ensure the contract they agreed to was intact. Meanwhile, Andre chatted quietly with Stanley and pretended not to watch Monica from the corner of his eye and think about his life's biggest regret.

Chapter Three

ndre Campos.

Monica hadn't seen him in *ages* and was ill-prepared to see him now, but somehow held her emotions in check.

After they signed the documents, there were handshakes all around. When it came time to shake Andre's hand, Monica held her breath and met his gaze with direct eye contact.

Stay strong, she silently coached herself.

Last time she saw him he had cornrows, but now his hair was cut in a neat style close to his scalp. He had one of those rough-hewn faces, exacerbated by a pale patch of skin slicing through his eyebrow, the result of a childhood accident when he fell off his bike and hit his head.

Time slowed to a crawl, almost coming to a standstill. The rapid motion of her fluttering heart shortened her breath and made her a little dizzy. Touching hands sent a bolt of electric shock through her. She hid her reaction with two solid pumps before tugging away her fingers, but the quick removal of contact did little to quell the tingling in her palm.

Nine years should have been long enough to recover from their breakup. Yet she couldn't forget how he'd made her feel and the almost forbidden nature of their relationship—Monica coming from a wealthy background while Andre came from a family with an intimate knowledge of the criminal justice system. His father had laundered money for a local gang before he died, his mother was serving time for killing her abusive boyfriend, and Andre himself had been in and out of juvenile detention centers before moving to Atlanta to live with an uncle.

After a brief consult, Penelope said goodbye and Stanley escorted her from the room, which left Monica alone with Andre. As agreed to before she arrived at Chambers Enterprises, and mentioned again during the short meeting, she was supposed to visit Midnight Lounge and take photos during the pre-opened stage. She'd have to go there with Andre instead of Nigel, and she wasn't so sure she wanted to.

Making a show of checking her phone bought her time. She didn't know what excuse to give, but she did *not* want to go to the property with Andre. He made her nervous and on edge.

"Any emergencies that would keep you from going to the restaurant now?" His voice splintered the tension in the room, low and smoky, the tone reminiscent of a chain smoker sprinkled heat on her skin, and every word he uttered sounded sexy.

Monica lifted her eyes from the phone. If she didn't know better, she'd say he was being sarcastic.

His skin was a shade lighter than hers. More often than not, his dark eyes remained slightly narrowed, which gave him a brooding appearance—as if always studying and assessing the person he spoke to. But when he smiled, he transformed in a breathtaking way.

Broad-nosed with a square jawline, his masculine features were accessorized with a chin puff, the only hair on his face.

17

"I don't see anything that needs my immediate attention," Monica said, tucking the phone in her purse. "I'm ready."

He didn't move and watched her for a beat. "So, you're a social media influencer. Why am I not surprised?"

She smiled faintly. "I floundered for a bit and sort of fell into it."

"How does a person 'fall into' being a social media influencer?"

"When you document your life online and people follow you to see what you're going to post each day. Believe me, I'm as shocked as anyone." She shrugged.

Most people assumed she simply posted pictures, but she'd learned a lot from being part of a family of entrepreneurs. Her income was diversified. She owned several income-generating properties around the country and a percentage of a tequila company.

"At least you were able to put those marketing classes to use."

She gave a dry laugh. "Hardly. Everything I've learned came from real life experiences or someone else teaching me or mentoring me. If I had to do it all over again, I'd probably skip college. I haven't used any of that stuff. What about you?"

His eyebrows lifted higher. "What about me?"

She swallowed as tension bloomed in her stomach. "Did-did you finish?"

He shook his head. "Nah."

Her heart broke. Andre had been the first person in his family to go to college and earned a full tuition scholarship to boot. "I figured by now—"

"Nah." He checked his watch, cutting off further conversation. "If we're going to see the inside of the building, we should go to beat the lunch time traffic."

"You know... maybe I should visit the restaurant another day."

"Don't you need pre-opening photos to start promoting?"

"I can take those tomorrow or in a few days."

His eyes narrowed more. "The contract says you're supposed to put out the first post within twenty-four hours of signing the contract. You don't want to come with me, fine, but you need to adhere to the terms. Unless you're reneging on the contract?"

"That's not what I said."

"That's what I'm hearing, otherwise why wouldn't you want to come with me now?" he asked, his voice a challenge.

He raised one eyebrow, and her lips tightened. No way would she allow him to think she had any kind of hang up on him still.

"I needed to check my phone for messages and notifications while we were busy in the meeting, but now I'm good. I'm ready, if you are."

He hesitated, as if he didn't quite believe her, then he asked, "Where'd you park your car?"

"I didn't drive."

"Then you can ride with me."

"That's not necessary, I can call a car."

"We're going to the same place, Monica."

She opened her mouth to argue and then closed it. Whatever argument she came up with didn't make sense. They *were* going to the same place, so declining sounded ridiculous.

"Right," she said.

"I'm parked out back."

She followed him out the conference room, biting her top lip as her gaze spanned the width of his shoulders beneath the dark jacket. At 5'8, she towered over most women when she wore heels and stood above a lot of men. Andre was taller, though she came close to eye level with him in her current heeled sandals. Heat crawled up her neck as she drank him in. Damn, he had such a sexy walk. His Denzel Washington walk —slow, smooth, and exuding supreme confidence.

He stopped at the receptionist desk and let them know he and Monica were headed to the property. Then he held the door open for her, and she slipped out, casting her eyes downward as she brushed past.

They went behind the building to what she initially thought was a black Escalade. Instead, it was a deep, dark purple.

"I've never seen a purple Escalade before. Custom job?" she asked.

"Yeah."

He used to drive an old Cadillac in college, but she remembered him always saying his dream vehicle was an Escalade. He'd bought one—brand new, it seemed. Not cheap, which meant he must be doing very well for himself.

When he started the SUV, rap music blared through the speakers.

"Shit. Sorry about that." He immediately lowered the volume but didn't turn off the music.

Within minutes, they hit the highway, Andre driving one-handed, two thick gold rings flashing on the middle fingers curled around the steering wheel. Oddly enough, the sizable vehicle seemed extra small with his large frame resting in the driver's seat. Monica sat up straight, legs crossed away from him and trying to take up as little space as possible, practically pressing her body into the door.

Her body remembered his, and her core throbbed and ached from the memories. The weight of him on top of her. His gruff voice in her ear. Strong fingers encircling her wrist and pinning her to the mattress.

Growing up she'd always been self-conscious about her figure. She never developed the voluptuous hourglass curves extolled in the songs she listened to. Instead, she'd been gangly and tall for her age, taking after her father in height. She never gained weight and remained thin, never developing a big booty or breasts, and her hips were practically nonexistent.

Over time, she developed more confidence and became more comfortable in her skin, capitalizing on the way her slender figure allowed her to wear haute couture, and chose to display her personality in outlandish outfits that worked well on social media and made her followers envious.

Andre had never made her feel like a shapeless entity. With him, she became womanly, and the way he used to look at her made her heart rate triple its beat, a long time ago. Back in college, when they were much younger and naive.

Before he broke her heart and shattered her trust.

Chapter Four

"**H**ere we are."

Andre pulled in front of the building and parked. The 17th Street Hotel was a boutique hotel situated in a prime location inside the Perimeter—Highway 285—which circled Atlanta. Only five stories, it offered personalized service for the discerning traveler.

Andre and Monica stepped out of the vehicle onto the circular driveway designed with a cobblestone surface, its old-world charm a striking contrast to the modern, black exterior of the hotel.

"The restaurant." Andre pointed to the right of the main building at the one-story addition. "At night, the doors and windows are rimmed in blue light."

"Attracts attention," Monica commented.

"Exactly."

"I don't remember the rooftop space from the original information Nigel's assistant sent over."

"The idea evolved over time. Come on, and I'll show you inside."

Andre led her down a paved path hugged by manicured shrubs on either side.

"People can enter from inside the hotel or out here," he said, grasping the bronze handles on the door and pulling it open. He allowed Monica to precede him, and as she passed, he breathed in the sensual, musky fragrance which had tortured him in the Escalade. An unfamiliar scent, it was quintessential Monica—brash, strong, and attention-getting.

Inside, two workers added finishing touches. One man touched up the crimson paint on the wall, while another perched on a ladder screwing a lightbulb into a wall sconce.

"Hey, Lloyd, Jones," he called out.

They called back a greeting, waving their hands and planting curious eyes on Monica as she strolled in with him. He couldn't blame them. She had the graceful, elegant walk of a model and the features to match.

After a few feet, Andre came to a stop. "To the left, the entrance to the hotel, and this is the bar," he announced.

"Beautiful," Monica almost whispered. Her fingertips lightly caressed the polished, dark-stained wood of the bar, already fully stocked with high-backed stools in front.

On the right, leather chairs surrounded tables in a line against the wall. Guests could see all the way to the back, where the space opened into additional tables, behind which a small stage would house a DJ.

Monica turned in a slow circle to capture all the features. "I like everything I'm seeing so far. I'm getting great ideas for when I bring in my team for the photo shoot. "

"Looks better at night with all the lights. Let me show you the rooftop."

Andre walked toward her, and she edged away by sidestepping him. He noticed she kept her distance. She'd practically been glued to the car door when they rode over together, which meant she felt "it"—the energy vibrating between them. It created tension in his neck and spine.

Andre led the way across the Brazilian cherry hardwood floors to the stairs beside the stage. A metal handrail took them to the second floor where more tables and chairs overlooked the entire restaurant. "Offices are up here," he explained, pointing to the closed doors marked *Employees Only*.

He pushed open an Exit door and led the way up a winding staircase, which led to the rooftop. Hotel rooms from the upper floors looked onto the outdoor space, providing free advertising to entice guests to come visit.

"Nice view," Monica crooned, her voice dropping low, her lips extending into a smile.

Andre watched her. Couldn't keep his eyes off her. Wanted to put his hands on her.

She stepped across the rooftop, which contained a smaller bar and tables sandwiched between Robin-egg-blue sofas. A railing ran around the perimeter.

"This is going to be nice when it opens." She turned to him, her chestnut eyes bright.

Andre stuffed his hands in his pockets. "I agree. Chambers did a good job."

"Did you help with any of this?"

"Nigel has his own design people, but I contributed suggestions."

"Did they incorporate any of them?"

"This, actually, was my idea. People like to dine out when the weather is nice, and Georgia has plenty of days for people to enjoy during the year."

"More than New York, I'll bet," she said with a smirk.

"Nice weather is the only advantage Georgia has over New York," he shot back.

They always used to debate which city was better—New

York or Atlanta.

She gave him a full on smile then. Damn, she was beautiful.

"How did you end up working with Nigel?"

"Long story."

"I have time."

He arched an eyebrow, surprised by her curiosity. "I started small, actually. Worked as a host at one of his lounges, making sure people were comfortable and enjoying themselves. Then I became the floor manager at his club on the east side. It's an older crowd but his most successful."

"Because of you?"

"I wouldn't say all that. He was sure as hell making millions before I came along, but he implemented some of my ideas. People want to have a full experience when they go out, so I suggested he add live entertainment—bands playing mellow music, comedians—to go with the excellent food and call the place a lounge. Sales skyrocketed." No point in acting humble. He was proud his suggestions resulted in increased revenue. "I had some money saved up and eventually he took me on as a partner. I've invested in three of his properties so far."

She raised her eyebrows. "Pretty impressive."

"I've been frugal and careful with my money," he said.

"I always knew you'd do great things."

Hearing her speak in that soft voice turned him inside out—and angered him. "Did you?"

"Of course. You're smart. You got a scholarship to the University of Georgia."

"Lucky me, right?"

She glanced away.

He shouldn't have hinted at the past but couldn't help himself. He started college a year late and met Monica when they were both sophomores in the same geography class. Right away, he became impressed with her Spanish language skills.

Despite having an Afro-Nicaraguan father, Andre barely spoke Spanish because his parents hadn't wanted him to get confused growing up. Meanwhile, she grew up in a bilingual household because of her stepfather and stepbrothers.

He and Monica studied together and became friends. Within months, their friendship became more than a mere friendship. When she found out about his mother's life sentence for killing his abusive boyfriend, she hadn't judged. In fact, she'd been sympathetic. When she learned about his own checkered past hustling, fighting, and stealing cars, she'd been intrigued.

His bad boy image kept her attention, while her fun-loving rich girl antics kept him enthralled. They were more than opposites. They were two stars on a collision course, destined for hurt but too young and foolish to recognize the signs.

Facing away from him, Monica rested her hands on her waist, arms akimbo. "I've seen enough. I'll shoot a video and take some pictures I can use on my page and in my Instagram stories to tease the opening."

Andre heard her but his attention was elsewhere. His gaze traveled the length of her body from her feet upward, snagging on her short hair and how it tapered to the graceful line of her neck.

"Why'd you cut your hair?" he asked.

Monica smoothed a hand from her crown to her nape. "Why? You don't like it?"

"It looks fine. I think it fits your personality, actually."

A smile pulled at the corners of her lips but didn't come to fruition. If there was one thing he knew, Monica Connor liked to be complimented. Not out of any sense of vanity, though. Oddly enough, she used to be self-conscious about her looks.

"Too much maintenance," she answered.

"You always did complain about having to take care of your hair. 'It's too much trouble.'" He spoke in a whiny voice.

Her eyes widened. "I don't talk like that!"

"Yeah, you do."

"Well, doesn't matter. It's gone now and I'm happier." She shrugged, all cute.

"Monica Connor always does whatever she wants," he said, resting a forearm on the iron railing. He didn't want to leave. He wanted to prolong their time together.

"Always," she said with a jutted chin.

Andre let out a brief laugh. Same old Monica. "Where do you want to take the video? You should definitely get the seating arrangement and the view of the buildings in the background," he said, pointing out the relevant spots.

Monica gasped. "You still have it," she whispered.

At first he didn't know what she was talking about, but then he caught how her gaze fixated on his wrist. When he had lifted his hand, his jacket slid back and revealed two intertwined hearts etched into the skin on the inside of his right wrist. Though he'd gestured with his hands all day, she hadn't noticed because she'd always been on the other side where she couldn't see the symbol.

Andre gazed down at the tattoo. He'd had it for so long, he'd forgotten it was there, and it was tiny compared to others on his body. "I do."

Then his eyes met hers, asking the question without actually asking. Did she still have hers? Like a mind reader, Monica pulled back the sleeve of her jacket and flipping her arm displayed the inside of her left wrist. Two red hearts, one smaller than the other, locked together.

Nostalgia, regret, anger, beat down on him all at once.

They'd gotten the tattoos at the same time, when their love had seemed infinite. They agreed the sign represented the depths of their feelings for each other. Simple red hearts etched into their skin. The identical mark would bind them together forever. A symbol of their never-ending love. At least, that's what it was meant to be.

Forever with you ain't enough, he had whispered.

"For ever and ever," Monica said in a low voice, the same words she said right before they kissed inside the tattoo parlor.

His chest tightened with emotion, and suddenly he no longer wanted to be on the rooftop. He wished to be anywhere else but here, with her. The softness in her eyes had been his downfall and now slowly killed him with the memory of all that he'd lost.

Sweet, crazy Monica. Wild. Untamed. A free spirit. The woman he had been willing to do anything for. Sacrifice anything for.

He realized with a start that the entire time he'd been with her, not once did he think about Belinda, and a wave of shame engulfed him.

"I'm engaged." He said the words as a reminder to himself, but they came out blunt and landed like an anvil, harsh after their brief trip down memory lane.

Her soft expression fell away. "What?"

"I'm engaged to Nigel's daughter—Belinda Chambers."

He might be crazy, but he could almost swear hurt filled her eyes, and he almost took back the words. Almost said, *I don't mean it.* Instead, he watched her fumble with her purse.

"Good for you. I'm going to do a 360 video. You should leave the roof."

She removed her phone, and Andre didn't move, angry at the cold that descended between them. A change *he* had initiated.

When she turned her back on him, he finally left the rooftop.

Chapter Five

Engaged.

The word cut with the sharpness of a sword.

Monica stood on the rooftop, unable to move after taking a panoramic video. She'd had to record the video five times because of her fake-looking smile the first four times.

Andre was engaged to marry someone else and would soon be off the market. Ever since he divulged that piece of information, a tight knot formed in her stomach and wouldn't go away.

Why did she care so much?

I don't, she thought to herself, straightening her shoulders and lifting her head. She dated plenty and lived a satisfying life. Poor Belinda was in for a rude awakening. Today she was engaged, tomorrow she might be single because Monica knew first-hand about the fickleness of Andre's affection. After months of expressing words of love, he'd dumped her. Her first real lesson in the heart-breaking nature of love.

She left the rooftop and made her way down the stairs. She found Andre with his back to the restaurant, head bowed and hands stuffed into his pockets.

He lifted his head. "All done?"

"For now. I'll return another day with lights, equipment, and a photographer to take images I can use to post a countdown before the opening. I'll talk to Nigel about it." With her photographer, Daisy, and the right equipment, she could take amazing shots to really show off the interior.

She sensed Andre's gaze on her, though she remained focused on her phone screen.

"So we're good to go?" he asked.

"All done," she confirmed.

They took the stairs to the first floor, and Andre said goodbye to the men on the way out. In the parking lot, he opened the passenger door, and Monica slid onto the seat. Her eyes followed him as he rounded the front of the Escalade to the driver's side.

She wanted to know more about his engagement. How long had he been engaged? What was his fiancée like? Probably nothing like Monica.

Andre climbed in and started the car. Neither spoke for several minutes as he maneuvered onto the highway.

"You and Nigel are going to make a lot of money at that restaurant," she said.

Andre drove with one hand draped over the wheel, the other resting on the gear shift. He used to place his hand on her thigh, warm and smooth, and sometimes he pushed higher to tease her while they idled in traffic.

"No doubt."

"What about you? You still want to open your own place?"

His dark eyes rested on her, and her heart juddered against her ribs, but she remained calm.

"Can't believe you remember that. I think about it sometimes. I drew up plans a while back."

"You did?"

He shrugged. "Yeah, sketches. Figure I'd have a hookah bar, a dance floor, and a... well, I have ideas. Who knows if they'll ever happen."

"If you work hard enough, you can make it happen," Monica said quietly. She'd always believed in his natural brilliance, and his success with Nigel demonstrated his business savvy. Her problems with him stemmed from the fact that he bailed, leaving her heartbroken, lonely, and no longer believing in love.

She should hate him, but instead her blood simmered. She didn't only want Andre's body. One of the reasons they had become close in school was because she found him easy to confide in. Their long talks and the way he listened without judgment had gotten her through rough days.

But their chemistry had been undeniable. His touch was scorched Earth, like a wildfire burning everything in its path, and she wanted nothing more than for him to caress her cheek, drop an affectionate kiss to her lips, or place his hand between her legs until he stroked her to ecstasy.

Goodness, what was wrong with her? She drew a trembling breath and gazed out the window at the moving traffic.

"Yeah, I could make it happen," Andre said absent-mindedly.

They fell quiet for another few minutes.

"So, you're engaged. To your partner's daughter."

"Yes."

The short, clipped response didn't deter her. If he didn't want to talk about the engagement, he shouldn't have mentioned it.

"You know what I find kind of odd?"

He glanced at her, eyebrows dipping lower over his eyes. "What?"

"You're engaged to someone like her. I believe you had a

31

problem with me and my family's mother, but now you're dating another wealthy woman. Kinda odd."

"I didn't have a problem with your family's money. We just weren't compatible."

"But you're compatible with her?"

"Yes."

Another shaft to the heart.

"Excuse me."

"You know what I mean, Monica."

"Yes, I do."

"No, you don't," he said.

"I do. I never asked you to take the blame for me, Andre. You chose to, because you said you loved me, and then you regretted it and became angry. The end."

"What the hell are you talking about? I was never angry with you, and I never regretted taking the blame."

"Right," Monica said.

After a year together, they had been inseparable, but the second semester of their junior year, someone ratted her out to the campus police. To this day, she didn't know who. Officers showed up in her room with Andre present. They found her weed, but Andre said it belonged to him. She argued but he shut her down, getting between her and the officers and insisted she was lying to protect him.

Cowardly and scared of the repercussions, she finally fell quiet. Initially, she thought the administration would only suspend him, but he lost his scholarship and was expelled. The day he was packing up to leave, she went to see him, and he broke up with her.

Andre turned in her direction, a frown between his eyes. "I'm telling you the truth."

"I don't believe you. *This* didn't mean anything to you." She held out her wrist to show the linked hearts. "Forever my ass."

"You don't know what you're talking about," Andre muttered, anger underlining the words.

"Then correct me. What am I wrong about?"

"I don't want to have a conversation about something an event from nine years ago."

"Why not?"

"Because it's over, Monica!"

"You owe me an explanation!"

She needed him to admit she screwed up and destroyed what they had and he'd never forgiven her though he'd claimed nothing could tear them apart. Like a young, naive fool, she'd believed him. Believed in their love. Reveled in their opposites attract story.

Andre swung the car off the highway onto the shoulder, and Monica gasped, gripping the door handle.

He slammed on the brakes, skidding in the gravel. Cars whizzed by them on the highway as he turned to face her.

"I don't owe you shit," he said, eyes flaring angrily at her. "I took the blame for you, and I accepted the repercussions of my decision, but that doesn't mean I want to talk about it now. Or ever."

Monica fingers gripped the edge of the seat, fighting the urge to cry like she'd done when he broke up with her. She was so tempted to humiliate herself. So tempted to beg his forgiveness.

"You hate me." Her voice cracked, and her throat burned with suppressed tears as she awaited his denial or confirmation.

Andre briefly closed his eyes and breathed slowly out his nose, clearly calming himself down. He opened his eyes again. "I could never hate you," he said in a quiet voice.

Was he telling the truth? That would be something, at least. She'd spent days in bed shedding tears of grief and loss long after he left her life.

Because of the tattoo, she never forgot what happened, but sometimes went weeks or months without remembering, and then the stark reality of what had occurred—what she'd allowed to happen, would return—with a vengeance.

She should have admitted the truth to the officers. She'd had more resources than he did, but she'd been afraid of the consequences. Afraid of disappointing her family. She wished she could turn back time. Even if they never stayed together, she hated knowing his dream of being the first in his family to graduate from college was destroyed because he protected her.

Andre checked the mirrors and then pulled into traffic. They rode the rest of the way to the Chambers building in complete silence.

Chapter Six

"**G**uess where I am?" Monica teased in a sing song voice. Her eyes flirted with the camera.

Andre sat in his office, watching her give a 360-degree view of Midnight's rooftop on Instagram. After additional teasing and promising her followers more to come, Monica puckered her lips and air-kissed the lens.

She signed off with her signature line. "Tah-tah, bitches." Then threw up the peace sign.

He knew her signature because he had spent almost two hours scrolling her page, reading posts and watching videos.

A car horn blared outside, and he glanced at the window. The waning light of early evening nudged the day toward darkness, and with the building so quiet, most, if not all, the staff must have already left.

"Shit." He had completely forgotten about dinner with Nigel and Belinda. Jumping out of the chair, he snatched his jacket from the coat rack and raced through the empty office.

With a bout of reckless driving, he arrived at Nigel's estate ten minutes late, and a member of the staff led him into the library where the older man was fixing himself a drink.

"Hello!" Nigel greeted him in a hearty manner. Almost from the first day Andre worked for him, they established a warm work relationship, long before Andre became involved with his daughter.

Brown-skinned, with short-cropped hair sprinkled with gray, Nigel looked distinguished in a simple mahogany, long-sleeved shirt and dark pants, perfectly placed wrinkles around the eyes, as if they'd been drawn on his face.

"I was about to call you. Thought you might have forgotten about us."

"Not at all." Andre strolled deeper into the room.

"Drink?"

"Sure. Rum and Coke."

Nigel fixed the drink and handed it over to Andre.

"How'd it go today?" Nigel settled in his leather recliner and lifted a gin and tonic to his lips.

Before Andre could answer, Belinda breezed into the room.

"Hello, Daddy." She cast a quick glance at Andre before bending to kiss her father on the cheek.

"Hello, angel." Nigel's face and voice softened the way it always did whenever he spoke to his daughter, his only child.

At the age of twelve, Belinda's parents divorced, and she chose to stay with her father rather than live with her mother. Based on their conversations, Andre suspected she arrived at that decision because of her mother's strict rules, whereas her father let her do whatever she wanted. She had him eating out of her hand.

Belinda turned in a circle, hands on her hips. "What you think?"

A mustard colored skirt hugged her generous behind—the first thing he noticed about her when they met—and a series of gold necklaces glimmered against a blue top. Raven hair swept down her back in a tumble of loose curls, framing her pretty, heart-shaped face.

"You look stunning, angel," Nigel said, with an indulgent smile.

"And the shoes?" Belinda kicked up one foot to show off the bejeweled stilettos on her feet.

"Stunning as well," Nigel said.

"You already know you look great, Belinda," Andre added.

"Thank you." A faint blush surfaced on her mocha-colored skin.

It was adorable he could still make her blush after almost two years together.

She walked over and gave Andre a peck at the corner of his mouth, casting a flirtatious glance up at him with eyes full of promise. The chaste kiss allowed her to show affection without creating an awkward situation in front of Nigel.

"Dinner almost ready?" Nigel asked.

Belinda nodded. "That's why I came to get you." She looped an arm through Andre's as the three of them left the library.

"How did the visit to the retail space go today?" Andre asked.

"I think we found a place, didn't we, Daddy?" She glanced back at her father.

"I think so. It needs a little work, but the location gets lots of foot traffic and is large enough to fit your needs, isn't it?"

"Definitely. Better than the others." She gazed up at Andre. "You have to come see it one day."

"You don't need my opinion. If you like it, and your father likes it, you have your spot." At her crestfallen expression, he added, "*But,* if you really want me to, I'll take a look."

Belinda's face brightened. "Thank you. You know how much I value your opinion."

They entered the large dining room, elegant with two chandeliers and a rectangular table covered with a white tablecloth, which easily accommodated fourteen people. They took their seats, the same positions as always. Nigel at the head of the table, Andre to his left, and Belinda across from him.

Andre spread a white napkin across his thighs. Eating at the Chambers residence was always an event, with multiple courses and a full table setting. A uniformed female member of the staff placed a plate of strawberry and spinach salad in front of each of them.

"You were going to tell me about the meeting today," Nigel reminded him.

Andre finished chewing before he answered. "Right. The meeting went well. Papers were signed and afterward Monica and I toured the restaurant, and she already posted the video."

"Good, good. What did you think about her?"

Andre hesitated. "I know her, actually."

"Who are we talking about?" Belinda asked. No surprise she suddenly became interested at the mention of another woman.

"Monica Connor. She's an influencer your father hired to promote the new restaurant."

Her eyebrows raised higher. "I know her. She's basically a party girl, always doing something fun and interesting. She's amazing! I'm a bit of a stalker." She let out a little laugh. "Her trip to St. John last year inspired me to take my girls' trip to the island. Remember when my friends and I went there over the holidays? So you know her?"

Andre nodded and lifted his glass of rum and Coke. They both drank wine, which he didn't care for. "Yeah, from way back."

"How do you know her?" Belinda asked.

Andre hesitated again. If he explained they used to date, then he'd have to explain everything that happened, including she was the woman who had inspired him to get the tattooed hearts on his wrist Belinda questioned him about in the past.

"We both went to the University of Georgia." He shrugged to downplay the importance of their relationship.

"Right, I forgot she went there," Belinda said.

His nonchalant attitude paid off, because Belinda didn't seem particularly interested in gleaning more information.

"Since we're talking about the restaurant, I was thinking, why don't you handle opening night?" Nigel smiled and set down his knife and fork.

"Me?" Andre asked, surprised. "What about J.L.?"

J.L., the other managing partner, oversaw the opening of new venues.

"He's taking a well-needed vacation around that time, and I think you could handle the opening. You know all about the business from when you worked as a floor manager at my other place. Essentially, this will be your baby. You're coming out of the shadows. You can take over from here and handle all the marketing with Ms. Connor and her team, if you're interested." Nigel laughed. "You're surprised."

According to rumors around the office, J.L. planned to retire soon and move closer to his grandchildren. Andre was no fool. This opportunity "to come out of the shadows" meant one thing—Nigel was setting him up to take J.L.'s place as a managing partner.

"I am a little surprised, but I can handle the added responsibility."

Andre glanced at Belinda, who smiled across the table at him before sipping her wine. Did she have anything to do with this?

"Ms. Jones has all the contact information, so you can get in touch with Ms. Connor and work on the ongoing promotion of the restaurant. Her fan base is exactly the demographic we want to cater to, so we need to make this young lady happy."

Andre nodded. He had zero interest in being a managing partner at Chambers Enterprises. His ultimate goal was to open his own lounge. For now, he invested and saved his money. Working with Monica would be a distraction, but he should be able to handle it. He had handled much worse in his life.

Throughout the rest of the evening, the dinner conversation progressed easily, with the conversation centering mostly on work—Belinda's shoe store and Midnight Lounge. All three lobbed ideas around the table until staff removed the dessert plates, and then Nigel excused himself.

Normally, Andre remained behind to spend time with Belinda, but he made up an excuse about being tired. He needed time alone, to think.

"I can't believe you know Monica Connor," she said in a casual tone, as they walked hand in hand to the door.

Andre didn't react. Belinda had a jealous streak and bringing up Monica again meant she was fishing for information.

"I get the impression you were more than friends." They stopped at front of the door, and she gazed up at him.

He decided to come clean. "Yeah, we were. She's an old girlfriend."

"So you lied."

"I didn't lie. I just didn't want it to be a thing."

"You made it a thing by not telling me."

Jeez, not now. An argument was the last thing he needed. "It was a long time ago. We were young."

Belinda folded her arms over her chest, sharp eyes studying him. "Why'd you break up?"

"I don't remember why."

"You don't?"

"No, I don't." He held fast to the lie and didn't flinch.

"Is she the reason you have the hearts tattoo?"

Damn, she was quick, but Andre kept his tone neutral. "Yes."

Belinda angled her head to the right. "Hmmm. Now I know her name."

"Our break up was a long time ago."

"Yes, it was." Belinda shrugged. "I'm sure I have nothing to worry about. She's flighty and—"

"She's not flighty."

She stared at him and he stared back. Monica actually ran a business. She was *not* flighty, and he wouldn't budge from the statement..

"Daddy really loves you, you know. He sees you as the son he never had."

Where the hell did that come from?

"I appreciate him and the opportunities he gave me."

She smiled slyly. "I think he wants to make you a managing partner. If he does, then you won't have to worry about your little project."

His 'little project' was the idea for his own lounge, but she didn't see the value in it, and he regretted discussing the project with her. If Belinda had one flaw, it was her self-centeredness. She wanted him to be excited about her business but didn't care one iota about his.

She raised up on her toes, wound her arms around his neck, and brought her lips close to his. "I'll let you go because I'm sure you had a long day. I love and trust you, and I'm not worried about a social media influencer with heart-shaped tattoos from your past."

Andre placed his hands on her hips. "Good. Because you have nothing to worry about."

"I know. She has nothing on me."

"And she's from my *past*, Belinda."

She searched his face and then smiled. They kissed warmly before she groaned and pushed him away.

"Go, before I sneak you upstairs."

Andre chuckled. They both knew she'd never do anything so bold. She might be grown, but this was still her father's house, and they never hooked up there. Only at Andre's place.

"Love you," she said.

"Love you."

After another quick peck on the lips, Andre jogged down the stairs and climbed into the Escalade. He drove off the property to the sound of Kendrick Lamar's latest track blasting through the speakers.

He considered how to navigate working with Monica on the promotion of the new restaurant. He also considered how, for the first time he could remember, he hesitated to say "I love you" to Belinda.

If there was one thing he was *not* going to do, it was allow his obsession with Monica Connor to mess up his life again.

Chapter Seven

Monica stared up at the ceiling as she lay in bed. She'd crept in late last night after sex with one of her regular hookups, in an effort to exorcise thoughts of Andre running through her mind.

Instead of an exorcism, she experienced a possession. The entire time she lay in another man's bed, all she could think about was Andre. His lips. The way his eyes crinkled when he smiled. The smoky richness of his voice. She became so wet and experienced such an Earth-shattering orgasm, she cried out and shuddered uncontrollably. Her partner had been shocked —shocked and mighty proud of himself, though her reaction had very little to do with him and everything to do with her vivid imagination based on memories.

She left his place in a cloud of guilt, needing to spend the night in her own bed because she couldn't stand the idea of cuddling while all she could think about was Andre, her new obsession.

Monica pulled on a pair of colorful capri leggings and a white tank and went downstairs.

"Good morning," she called, forcing a cheery note into her voice as she greeted Giselle, a member of the staff a few years younger than her. The young woman dusted the decorative items on the table in front of the three arches leading from the foyer into other parts of the house.

"Good morning," the young woman greeted back.

Monica strolled into the kitchen, expecting to see Rodolfo, the family chef. She found Rodolfo *and* her stepbrother, Bruno.

Monica let out a squeal of happiness. "Ahh! Bruno!" She flung herself into his arms and received a warm hug in return. "When did you get here?"

He'd been in Las Vegas for months opening his latest restaurant.

"I flew in last night on a red eye," Bruno said in lightly accented English. He inherited his father's gray eyes and good looks.

"You need a haircut, bro." Monica swept the tips of her fingers through his black hair.

"I should get a buzz cut like you," he teased.

"Not everybody can rock this," she said, smoothing a hand down her nape and doing a shimmy.

They both laughed.

"What are you doing *here,* at the house?"

"The renovations on my house aren't done," he replied, frowning in annoyance.

"Let me guess, Mommy said you could stay here."

"You know she did."

They both laughed again. Her mother was notorious for her desire to have the family around her.

"She's probably praying your place isn't ready for a long time."

Bruno chuckled. "I would not be surprised if she did."

"Good morning, Rodolfo," Monica greeted the chef.

Rodolfo was sprinkling seasoning over four steaks. He wore a gray cook's jacket and black trousers. Mexican, like her stepfather, he was middle-aged with warm brown eyes, pale skin, and dark hair.

"Good morning, Monica. Will you be joining your parents and Bruno for lunch?" he asked.

"I'm leaving in a few minutes to run some errands, so I won't be here for lunch," Bruno said.

"I'm going out for lunch," Monica replied.

She went to the refrigerator, a fifty cubic foot restaurant-size appliance with glass doors, which accommodated their large family and the huge platters of food they stored for the parties sometimes thrown there.

Monica lifted out the orange juice, which Rodolfo squeezed fresh every week. "Are you going to the store today?" she asked the chef, pouring herself a glass.

"Not until tomorrow. Do you need something?"

"We're running low on snacks. Could you pick up cookies, chips, that kind of thing?"

Rodolfo nodded. "Certainly. What would you like for breakfast?"

"I'm craving more of those delicious banana pancakes you made a few days ago."

"I'll whip some up for you," he answered, with a pleasant smile.

"*Gracias.* I'll be in the great room," Monica said, backing toward the door.

"I'll come get you when I'm finished."

"Bruno, I want to see your new house as soon as it's ready. I know the kitchen will be to die for."

"I'll call you first when I move in," he promised.

Monica left the kitchen and went toward the great room, the most popular room in the house. Juice in hand, she walked slowly into the high-ceilinged room. There was a fireplace and several conversational pockets created from the grouped sofas and armchairs.

Monica saw her stepfather, Benicio, lying on his back on the carpet in joggers and a T-shirt, one leg stretched out. In his sixties, his beard and mustache and the hair on his head had gone completely gray.

Her mother, Rose, knelt in front of him, holding the other leg aloft toward the ceiling. A mahogany-skinned woman barely over five feet, she wore her gray-streaked hair pulled back in a ponytail as she pushed the lifted leg toward Benicio's chest to stretch his hamstring.

"Your lower back bothering you again, Papa Ben?" Monica asked, taking a sip of her juice.

He winced and groaned out a yes as her mother applied pressure.

"One more," Rose murmured, and she pushed his leg again and held it in that position as she quietly counted.

Her mother then moved to the next leg. Dressed in sweats and a T-shirt, she maneuvered her much larger ex-husband as he groaned his relief at the pressure she applied.

In Monica's opinion, they had an odd relationship. Divorced but very friendly, which made her wonder why they didn't get back together. They obviously still cared about each other, because no one was fooled by her stepfather coming here to get his back stretched when he could afford a trainer to handle the issue for him.

She sat on the sofa in front of a table filled with wedding magazines and wrinkled her nose. There were so many. Multiple issues of *The Knot, Bridal Guide, Pretty Pear Guide, Inside Weddings, Brides, MunaLuchi Brides, and Southern Bride.*

Her eldest brother Ethan, whom she never believed would

marry again after a catastrophic first marriage, planned to tie the knot with his longtime live-in girlfriend, Skye. Since Skye's parents had passed away when she was a teenager, Rose filled the motherly role of helping Skye plan the wedding. Hence the wedding magazines. There had also been visits from two wedding planners and other activities, all of which Monica gladly excluded herself from.

Ethan had told Skye there was no budget, so Monica expected a grand affair. The first in the family since Audra— Monica's older sister—eloped when she married.

As far as Monica was concerned, marriage was an outdated institution. She couldn't imagine being tied down *one man* for the rest of her life.

Benicio and Rose finally stood up from the floor.

"How do you feel now?" Monica asked.

Resting his hands on his hips, Benicio smiled. "Much better than I did when I arrived. Your mother is a magician."

"Oh, please," Rose said, "It's just stretching, but I'm glad you feel better."

Benicio sat in an armchair, while Rose sat next to Monica.

"I'm surprised you didn't toss those in the trash," Rose said with amusement, her gaze switching to the magazines.

"I thought about it, but then decided you and Skye would probably lose your minds if you couldn't find them."

Her mother laughed and Benicio shook his head.

"How did the meeting go yesterday? I didn't get to talk to you last night."

"I came in late. Went well. I think this will be a spring board to more lucrative contracts. I signed the deal and then visited the restaurant they want me to promote. I... Everything went well."

"You were about to say something," Rose said. Her mother

was very perceptive. As a child, it had been hard to keep secrets from her.

Monica shrugged. "I... saw someone from my past. Do you remember Andre Campos?"

Rose's eyebrows lifted higher, and Benicio, who had been slouching in the chair, sat up straight.

"Where did you see him?" Rose asked.

"At the signing, actually. He's a partner at Chambers Enterprises."

"Do you have to work with him?" Benicio asked.

"No."

"Good," he said.

"It's been nine years. He's not the same person from college." The guilt from the past came back. Everyone believed Andre was the guilty party when in fact, it was her.

"How do you know he's not?"

"He seems different, that's all." She sipped her juice.

"Well, I'm glad you have so much confidence in him. I am not so sure."

"Benicio, people are allowed to change," Rose said.

"You need to be careful, Monica," Benicio warned, ignoring his ex-wife.

Monica laughed lightly. "I'm never going to see him again, so relax. I'm supposed to work with someone named John. Even if I did see Andre, I'm not young and dumb enough to fall for him again."

Benicio glanced at her mother.

Rose took a deep breath and covered Monica's hand resting on the sofa. "We know what kind of influence this young man had on you before. We want you to be smart and—"

Furious, Monica hopped up from the sofa. They acted as if she didn't have a brain to think for herself. Yes, she had spent all her free time with Andre. Yes, she had fallen apart when they broke up. She burst into tears at random times, stopped eating, and lost her zest for life. Only the counsel of her parents had kept her from crawling on her hands and knees and begging him to take her back.

"I'm not an idiot! And there's nothing for you to worry about because I won't be seeing him."

"Monica, watch your tone. Your mother is just concerned about you," Benicio said.

Her family knew Monica tended to like the bad boys, a preference which started in her teens. She hung out with them during her tomboy phase because they saw her as one of the guys. Unfortunately, her brothers—particularly Ethan and Bruno—guarded her like she was a delicate flower who needed protection the n'er do wells. Like having two fathers in addition to Papa Ben, but she didn't want protection.

At least Papa Ben had never been up in her business like her brothers, and fortunately for her, her brothers were preoccupied with their own lives now.

Monica took a calming breath. "All I'm saying is, I'm not the same person I used to be. I've had other relationships, and of course I'm not still hung up on him. Give me some credit."

"Okay," her mother said.

To further put their minds at ease, Monica added, "If I had feelings for him, it would be a waste of time. He's engaged to be married, to the daughter of the man he works for."

"Oh."

"So you see, you don't have anything to worry about."

Satisfied, Benicio returned to slouching in the chair. Her mother, however, gazed at her with uncertainty in her eyes.

"I'm going to check on breakfast and see how far Rodolfo has gotten with my pancakes."

Monica picked up her juice and left the room.

Chapter Eight

"Thank you," Rose said as a member of the staff cleared away the dishes. The weather hadn't become unbearably hot yet, so she and Benicio dined on the terrace overlooking the back of the property.

Benicio had spent the morning with her. After she stretched his lower back, they discussed repairs that needed to be done to the house. It was ridiculous that she practically lived alone—except for when Monica was at home—in such a big house, but he would not consider selling the property. Since she didn't work, he was responsible for all the maintenance and transferred additional funds into her account so she could pay the contractors when they arrived next week.

Sipping cold, refreshing lemonade, she watched him across the table as he checked his phone, a frown on his face.

"Something wrong?" she asked.

Benicio glanced up. "I received a text about an issue at the office. I'll take care of it when I go in this afternoon."

Oddly enough, when they were married, she seldom saw

him. Now they were divorced, he popped in during the day, something he never used to do before.

"So you're going into work this afternoon?"

"For a few hours." He set the phone on the table. "I need to fly to Mexico on business next week. You should come with me. It's been a while since you've visited."

"I'll think about it," Rose said, which was her polite way of turning down his offer. Spending time with his gregarious, welcoming family would be difficult in light of their divorced status.

"Do you plan to do any traveling this summer?"

"As a matter fact, I do. Sylvie invited me to join her for a couple of weeks on her yacht in the Greek islands."

Sylvie Johnson, a billionaire entrepreneur, took her multi-million dollar inheritance and built an greater fortune. She wasn't the kind of person to have a lot of friends, but she and Rose had become friendly in the past few years. They didn't have much in common, yet their relationship worked.

Benicio raised his eyebrows in surprise. "She invited you on vacation? What about Oscar?" he asked, referring to Sylvie's husband.

"He's coming too."

"So you'll be the third wheel?" Benicio asked, surprise in his voice.

Rose paused as she considered how to answer the question. "Not exactly. Sylvie—well, Oscar, really—also invited a friend."

Benicio's face blanked. "A male friend?"

Rose shifted in her chair. "Yes."

She and Benicio never discussed their dating status with each other. She assumed he dated, or at least had female companionship. She herself had gone out with a couple of men, but nothing serious. At her age, dating proved much more difficult than she'd anticipated. Most men in her age group were either married, going through a phase chasing much younger women, or uninterested in a woman whose ex-husband continued to take care of her financially. A set up provided a less stressful way to meet potential partners.

Benicio stared at her, and in the quiet she nervously lifted the lemonade to her lips and took a large gulp. There was reason for her to be nervous or ashamed, yet she was.

Finally, she replaced the glass on the table. "Ben, this is very awkward for me."

"You're dating?" he asked in a rough voice, his accent sounding thicker.

"I'm getting out there to see—"

"You're dating." No longer a question. A statement.

"Aren't you dating?"

He gazed out across the property before answering. "Here and there, nothing serious."

Rose swallowed the surge of pain that attacked her throat. She'd known, of course, but couldn't block her automatic reaction. The only way to get over him was to find someone new to love. They were both moving on. As they should.

"This isn't anything serious, either. I'm putting myself out there to see what happens," she said in a low voice.

Benicio continued to frown. The pleasant afternoon had been spoiled.

He stood abruptly. "I should go." He snatched up his phone and started walking away.

Rose jumped to her feet. "Ben—"

He stopped and turned toward her.

"Are you okay?" she asked softly.

A rueful smile crossed his lips before he answered. "Of course. Why wouldn't I be?"

She inhaled a pained breath and forced a smile. "No reason. I'm glad you're fine with this."

He didn't move. "We're divorced, which is what you wanted, right?"

No, it wasn't what she'd wanted. She'd wanted to spend the rest of her life with him, but he made it plain he didn't need her company. In turn, she became clingy and argumentative, drove a deeper wedge between them. In lieu of turning into bitter enemies, she asked for a divorce. He accepted.

Without another word, Benicio entered the house.

Rose slowly lowered into the chair. Her shoulders slumping. Her heart aching.

* * *

Pressing hard on the accelerator, Benicio muttered a stream of curses as he drove off the property. He dialed Oscar's number on the Bluetooth. The phone rang several times before his so-called friend picked up.

"Hello, old man. What are you doing calling me in the middle of the day?" Oscar asked in an upbeat voice.

"I found out you're a traitor."

"Excuse me?"

Benicio turned onto the back road toward the highway. "I left Rosa's a few minutes ago, and she informed me she's going on vacation with you and your wife and one of your male friends."

Oscar quietly cursed. "I was going to tell you."

"When exactly were you going to tell me that you were setting up my wife with one of your friends?"

"Ex-wife," Oscar corrected.

"Do not tell me what she is!" Benicio yelled with a burst of anger. He took a deep breath and forced himself to calm down. Despite being bilingual and living in the States for decades, he tended to lapse into Spanish when he became excited or upset.

"She is my wife. She will always be my wife," he growled.

"Ben—"

"How could you do this? We're friends. Didn't I have your back when you and Sylvie divorced and you were a depressed mess?"

"Yes," Oscar said in a weary voice.

"This is how you repay me?"

"Sylvie asked if I had a friend I could invite on the trip so Rose wouldn't feel like a third wheel. It's casual. Nothing serious."

"You invited another man on vacation with my wife. Casual or not, you have betrayed me."

"Benicio, will you calm down. I promise you, nothing is going to happen between them."

"How do you know this?"

"Because the person I invited is an old boating buddy of mine, and I'm pretty sure he's not Rose's type. He's nothing like you."

"You do realize she divorced me, no? Which means she's probably looking for a man who is *nothing* like me. I cannot believe you did this, Oscar." He slammed on the brakes and gripped the steering wheel. He almost rear-ended the car in front of him at the red light.

Mierda. He swiped trembling fingers across his brow. He needed to calm down before he ended up in an accident.

"What would you like me to do?" Oscar asked.

"I would like you to not do everything your wife asks you to do."

"Don't go there," Oscar said in a menacing tone.

"You know what, never mind. When is this trip?"

"She didn't tell you?"

"No, she didn't. As soon as she mentioned a vacation with another man, I lost my mind. I didn't ask any follow-up questions."

The car in front of him rolled forward and Benicio hit the gas.

"Fourth of July weekend. We're taking a couple of weeks off."

A few months away, which gave him plenty of time to plan.

"I'm coming too."

"What? You're not invited."

"Then invite me."

"Benicio, think about what you're doing."

"I am thinking about it, and I love the Greek islands. It's been years since I've visited, and it's long overdue. You're my friend, and you can invite me, can't you?"

Oscar muttered something unintelligible. "Rose is going to see right through this ruse. Anyone can."

"I. Do. Not. Care. I'm coming on the trip." His fingers tightened around the steering wheel.

"Let me ask you something. You told me Rose wanted a divorce because you never spent any time with her. Vacations were few and far between. Now she's moved on and is about to take a two week vacation, you suddenly can take off work?"

Benicio refused to acknowledge the very valid point his friend was making. "Tell your wife there's another person coming on this trip."

"You're behaving like an old fool, Benicio."

"Just do it. It's the least you can do for after stabbing me in the back."

"You want to embarrass yourself, fine. Join us on the trip with your ex-wife and see how well that goes."

"Thank you."

Benicio hung up the phone and pressed hard on the accelerator. He needed to get to work right away. There were projects he needed to wrap up, and he needed to let the staff know he was taking a vacation in a few months—his first vacation in years.

Chapter Nine

Monica succumbed to curiosity and found Belinda Chambers's Instagram account, which she scrolled through as she reclined on the bed against her mountain of pillows. Belinda had long black hair and a curvy body, the exact opposite of Monica. Their differences stung. Was she what Andre preferred?

Daisy entered the bedroom, struggling under the weight of two large paper sacks with handles and her messenger bag thrown across her body, while carrying Monica's large smoothie in one hand.

She lifted her eyebrows in surprise. "You cut your hair."

Daisy set down the items and turned in a slow circle so Monica could see her tapered pixie cut. "What do you think?" Nervous about Monica's opinion, her brow wrinkled.

"I love it, of course. Why'd you do it?" Monica asked.

"You inspired me," Daisy replied. "Last night I was reviewing your Instagram page in preparation for this meeting, and I took another look at the post where you cut off your hair. You captioned it "Freedom," and everyone was so supportive, I said to myself, you know, I want freedom too. I found some photos on Pinterest and showed my hairdresser. She matched the one I liked perfectly." She shrugged, a bright smile on her face.

"Good for you. How do you feel?"

"Amazing. Thanks for the idea."

Monica grinned. "You're welcome." Monica scooted off the bed and went to sit at the table near the window. Crossing her legs, she sipped the green smoothie Daisy brought her. *Delicious.*

"Now I have to figure out how to get a man," Daisy grumbled.

"I can't help you with that."

"Since I've been working with you, you've always had a man in your life. How do you meet them?"

"You actually have to leave the house," Monica said, hiking up one eyebrow.

Daisy let out an embarrassed laugh. "I guess that's an important step."

"Very important. Like I told you before, you're not going to meet men holed up in your apartment. Get out there and be seen. Go where the men are."

Daisy released an audible sigh. "I don't know if it's worth the effort. I can't seem to get relationships right. I always fall for the wrong men."

"You should expand your manhunting zone so you have a better chance of meeting the right one. Ohmigosh, you know what! Come with me to the opening of Midnight Lounge."

Daisy's eyes opened to the size of coasters. "Me? I wouldn't have anything to wear."

Monica cast a critical eye at her drab appearance—jeans, a gray T-shirt, and dirty tennis shoes. There was no need for her to dress up on a typical day while handling Monica's errands and other affairs, but for the opening, she'd have to do better—much better than anything Monica had seen her in since they met.

"You can borrow an outfit from my closet," she said.

"No, I couldn't." Daisy shook her head vehemently.

"I insist."

"I'm two sizes bigger than you."

"Not all my clothes are fitted. I'm sure we could find something for you to wear. If we don't, we're going shopping," Monica said.

"I don't know..."

"It's not a suggestion, it's an order. As my assistant, I'm ordering you to come with me to the opening, and I'm supplying the outfit. You deserve it for putting up with me. I don't want to hear another word about it, understand?"

Daisy giggled. "Yes, ma'am."

Monica grinned. "Perfect. Now, let's get to work. First thing, I need you to take my Porsche to the dealership. There's a check engine light on the dashboard."

Daisy dragged the bags closer and sat down. She removed an electronic tablet from the messenger bag and made a notation. "Got it. Okay, let's see what we have for today and the rest of the week..." Her eyes scrolled down the screen.

Monica received lots of invitations to events, as well as free merchandise from companies that wanted her to promote their products. Daisy helped her sort through them all. Correspondence and products were shipped to the coworking space she rented, where she went whenever she needed a creative boost or wanted to work distraction-free.

"You don't have anything else until five o'clock this afternoon because this afternoon's luncheon was canceled. Tomorrow, you do have a meet-and-greet sponsored by CamTam cosmetics." She removed a folder from the messenger bag and handed an embossed invitation to Monica. "There'll be approximately twenty-five influencers there, including you, salespeople available to answer questions, and makeup artists on hand if you want to try the products on site. At the end you'll receive a bag of samples to take with you."

"Looks like they're feeding us," Monica murmured, eyes on the invitation.

"Yep. Lunch is included. Flip over the invitation and you'll see the planned menu."

Monica hummed her approval at the list of delicacies, which included caviar. "What else do we have going on this week?"

Daisy removed a box from one of the shopping bags, and Monica squealed in delight.

"Yassss!" She snatched the shoebox from her assistant.

Her favorite shoe brand, Mignonne, mostly sold online and never failed to remember her when they produced a new heel they knew she'd like. Their shoes were pretty and comfortable, and before her deal with them, she had endorsed them on her social media handles. One photo in particular—with her legs crossed as she sat on the hood of a Bentley—had captured their attention and prompted them to make the initial contact. Ever since then, she received free shoes and they invited her to all their promotional events, including the grand opening of their first and only store at Lenox Square Mall.

She and Daisy reviewed her additional appointments, including a few sit down meetings and a scheduled photo shoot in the park, where she would promote a newly opened juice shop by extolling the nourishing and hydrating benefits of the drinks.

In the middle of their conversation, the phone rang, and she frowned at the screen. "It's Chambers Enterprises."

"What do you think they want?" Daisy asked, pulling more freebies from the bag at her feet.

"I have no idea. I hope there hasn't been a change." Could Andre have sabotaged the deal in some kind of retaliatory measure?

"Do you want me to answer it?" When she didn't want to be bothered, Daisy answered calls and responded to texts on her behalf.

"No. I'll handle it." She hit the green button. "Hello?"

"Hi, Monica, it's Andre."

Her core clenched, and she inhaled sharply at the unexpected sound of his low voice.

"Hi," she said cautiously. Daisy watched her.

"I need to tell you about a change of plans regarding Midnight. Nigel wants me to take over opening the restaurant, which means—"

"You'll be my point of contact," Monica interrupted.

"Exactly." Pause. "Are you going to be able to work with me?"

She bristled. "Are you going to be able to work with *me?*" she countered.

"I asked you first," he said.

Two days ago she'd been relieved she wouldn't have to see Andre again. With this change, she wasn't sure how to react but couldn't let him know how much his announcement affected her.

She glanced at the linked hearts on the inside of her wrist and clenched her jaw. She was Monica Connor. Tough and able to handle anything.

"I don't see an issue," she said in a cool tone.

"Neither do I."

"We're on the same page then. We can work together, no problem."

"No problem here."

Their stilted words sounded disingenuous, proving they were both liars.

"I've been reviewing the plan your team and Nigel came up with and wanted to discuss some other ideas."

"The contract has been signed, which states explicitly what I'll post and when," she reminded him, rising to her feet. He made her so antsy, she couldn't sit still. She crossed to the rug thrown across the gleaming wood floor.

"I'm not asking you to make major changes. We could finalize dates and incorporate a couple of ideas I have that complement what you already have planned."

She paused with her back to Daisy. "I guess I could do that," she said slowly.

"Are you free to come into the office on Monday, to discuss my ideas?" Andre asked.

"I don't usually get involved with the day to day details. My assistant, Daisy, will meet with you, and she'll relay the changes to me."

She turned to Daisy, who raised an eyebrow at the lie. Monica ignored her. Limited communication with him was best.

"Aren't you the decision-maker?" Andre asked.

"I am."

"Then you and I should talk."

Monica bit down on her molars. She hated how Andre challenged her. She didn't want to be anywhere near him again.

"Fine. I'll be there. Anything else?" she asked in a curt voice.

"No. I'll email you the details."

"Good." She hung up, not bothering to waste time with pleasantries.

"Who was that?" Daisy asked.

"Andre."

"Your *ex*?"

Monica had confided in her about her past relationship with Andre. She nodded, and went back to the table. Lifting her smoothie, she took a sip.

"What did he want?"

Retaking her chair, Monica explained about his request to discuss a few changes.

"The roll out has already been decided, though," Daisy said.

"I know, but he said he doesn't want any major changes."

"Still... maybe this is something Penelope should handle."

"It'll be fine," Monica said dismissively, heart racing.

"Are you sure that's how you want to handle this?" Daisy asked.

Monica remained silent for a moment. "No," she admitted. "But that's what I'm going to do."

Then pray her nerves could withstand being close to Andre.

Chapter Ten

Monica strolled into the Chambers Enterprises building with her head high. She'd taken extra care with her appearance. Wearing a floral black, backless romper that tied around her neck, she paired the outfit with strapless two-inch heels that showed off her toes, newly painted in the color buttercream like her fingernails, after a weekend mani-pedi.

Andre might belong to someone else, but a little part of her wanted him to see what he'd given up in college. She was successful and pretty and confident.

"Good morning. I have a ten o'clock with Andre Campos," she greeted the female receptionist, a young woman with red hair and bright green eyes.

"Your name?"

"Monica Connor."

The young woman checked her computer. "Yes, I see the appointment. Andre is waiting for you in the small conference room. I can take you there."

As she moved to come around the desk, Monica forestalled her with a raised hand. "No need. I know where it is."

"You're sure?"

"Absolutely. Thanks."

She made her way down the hall to the small conference room, heart galloping faster with each step closer. The blinds were closed for privacy, so she didn't see Andre until she entered the open door. He sat at the table with an open laptop and documents spread out before him, looking as handsome and inviting as when she'd seen him last week.

Monica swallowed the tightness in her throat as he came to his feet. Black shirt, gray tie, and black slacks on his slim hips. In addition to the rings, he wore a thick rope bracelet on his wrist. God, he was sexy. She was already moist from the sight of him.

Jaw tight, his dark gaze raked her from head to toe, piercing all the way to her soul. She experienced a tingling in her loins and a sense of satisfaction as his pink tongue swiped his lower lip, a familiar move that meant he was aroused.

"Hi," she said.

"Hi." He dragged his eyes away from her. "I guess we better get started."

"Before we get started, I have one request."

"Which is?"

"Can we call a truce? There's no reason for us to have animosity toward each other."

His eyes narrowed slightly, as though he suspected she had an ulterior motive. "I don't have any animosity toward you. Matter of fact, I figured you were the one upset about seeing me."

"I thought you were upset to see me."

He observed her in the intense way he had, while his forefinger tapped the top of the table. "Guess we were both wrong. So we can get along?"

"I'll give it a shot if you do," Monica replied.

A slow smile spread across his lips, and her heart went crazy. When he smiled, it was as if he was doing you a favor—blessing you.

"Let me guess, you've decided you need to stay on my good side."

He was too smart for his own good.

"I'm no dummy. As my contact, you're the man in charge at the moment. It's in my best interest for us to work well together."

"And you might need a referral in the future, and a referral from Chambers Enterprises would carry a lot of weight."

Instead of admitting he was right, Monica simply smiled and sat across from him. "What do you have for me?"

Andre retook his seat and scooted papers across to her. "Let's talk about ideas for promotion, leading up to opening night. I want this to be a strategy session where we brainstorm ideas. Nothing's off the table."

Monica folded her hands on the glass top and looked him steadily in the eyes. "Do you trust me?"

Andre sat back and tossed a pen on the table. "Listen, this is a big deal. I want the opening to be a success. So while I do trust you, I need to be actively involved in what you're doing."

"Did Nigel not explain how this works?"

"What do you mean?"

"For my static posts, I use a social media tool I'll give you access to, so you can approve my drafts. After your okay, I post. As for the opening being a success, you have nothing to worry about. The reason I'm so successful is because I do more than get mere likes on my posts. I get *engagement*—shares, comments, conversations among my followers. They trust me.

They know I won't recommend anything I don't believe in. So if I recommend Midnight Lounge, I guarantee you'll have a good turnout. To prove it, I have an idea." She leaned closer. "Give me a code I could use, for my followers, that'll give them a discount on a drink or an appetizer—or hell, the first drink free. Whatever you want to do. They'll give the code at the door, and they're handed a discount card. Makes me look good, but the added bonus is, the number of cards you give out will give you an idea of how many people showed up based on my marketing."

"You sound pretty confident."

"I've been doing this for a while."

"Okay, Miss Social Media Influencer, what else do you have planned?"

His teasing tone made her nipples tighten, but Monica stayed on task to lay out her ideas. "A live stream on opening night. For people who considered coming but headed home, if they see me having fun, you'll get a few more bodies in to the lounge because they won't want to miss out. FOMO at its best."

"Huh." Andre glanced at the papers on the table and then returned his attention to her. "I don't know shit about social media."

"You don't have an account anywhere?" She'd already checked but wanted confirmation.

Andre shook his head. "Never interested me."

"Well, that's why you have me. I love it and know how to leverage the platforms to make us both money."

"What other ideas do you have for promotion, leading up to the event?"

They discussed a good time for her to return to the lounge to take photos and shoot videos with her team—all to generate excitement about the opening. She explained how she would cross post to her Twitter account, which currently had over one million followers, to maximize exposure.

"You should be in one of the videos," she said.

"No thanks, I don't want to be out there like that."

"I'm going to change your mind."

"You won't," he said, voice firm.

"Andre, you're missing out on a great opportunity here. You're a fairly attractive guy."

"Fairly?"

She shrugged but continued. "I'm saying, you could use your appearance to draw women to the venue."

"Oh really?" He folded his arms across his chest, settling in for her explanation.

"Need I remind you about the bachelor auction?"

Flinging his head back, he let out a low groan.

She had convinced him to participate in a bachelor auction organized by her sorority, Sigma Gamma Rho, whose commitment to community service was embodied in their slogan, "Greater Service, Greater Progress." The auction raised funds for the March of Dimes, while the canned goods required as an audience entrance fee were collected and donated to a local food bank.

Monica laughed. "Come on, it wasn't that bad."

"Your sorors treated us like pieces of meat."

"Well, you were strutting around half naked in front of a bunch of women, and it wasn't only sorors, by the way."

"You're right. I remember Dean Myers bidding on that one guy—the football player. Can't think of his name right now." He frowned in concentration.

"Oh, I know who you're talking about." Monica paused to think, but the name wouldn't come to her. "Darn, I can't remember, but she started the bidding at five hundred dollars!"

Andre chuckled. "He looked panicked."

"He was. But he didn't go for the most money. You did."

Andre's eyes met hers. "Because of you. You got in a bidding war with the one girl—the one from our biology class. Considering the bidding started at fifty bucks, a thousand dollars was overkill."

Monica had never liked her. She always believed she had a thing for Andre. The way she eyeballed him, the way she giggled way too hard at his jokes.

She shrugged. "She wouldn't give up after we reached three hundred dollars, and I was not going to let her have you. Besides, it was for a good cause." She would have paid ten thousand if necessary. No way she was letting that chick go on a date with her man.

"I'd still like to know where these women got all that money from in college."

She let out a little laugh. "You'd be surprised. I'm sure some of them called home to their daddies and mommies."

"Like you, huh?"

"I didn't have to call home for a thousand dollars. That's play money," Monica quipped.

"Oh, it's like that."

She blushed. "No, it's not. I mean—"

"I know. You got the money. You never flaunted it. You do now though."

"Things are different now. I'm older and showing off my lifestyle is a way for me to *make* money. I don't make the rules, but I take advantage of them."

"You're lucky," he said.

"I know." She fell silent for a bit, unsure if she should share this story with him. "I was little, so I don't remember much about how my mom struggled before she met my stepfather. We have pictures, though." She stared down at her yellow fingernails. "We had this little apartment, and I remember the sounds of gunshots outside and loud music late at night. Everybody says there's no way I could remember because I was only two or three, but I remember. It's not a planted memory. I used to sleep in the bed with my mother, and the noise scared me, and she would hold me tight and sing to me to get me to stop crying. What I don't remember is what happened to make us move, but I've heard the story. One day we came home from the grocery store, and we had been robbed. My mother crumbled to the floor and started sobbing. It broke her, I guess. She'd been trying so hard, you know, after my dad died. That was the last straw." Her eyes blurred with tears at how her mother must have struggled with three little kids. She lifted her gaze to Andre, whose eyes had never left her.

"What happened afterward?" he asked quietly.

Monica cleared her throat. "She called my uncle, and by the weekend we were living with him and his wife. It wasn't ideal, but it was safer. Eventually, she met Papa Ben, and the rest is history."

"You never told me that story."

"I don't tell a lot of people. It's so long ago, I don't think about it much, to be honest. But um, I guess I wanted you to know I'm grateful for everything I have. I don't take anything for granted. I could sit around all day and do nothing, but I work hard, really hard at looking like I do nothing all day. And I get paid for it. I do what's necessary to support myself, even though I don't have to. Because I never want to be stuck like my mom was."

If a pin dropped in the quiet room, it would clatter like glass breaking on tile.

She had never admitted her fear to anyone, and she lowered her gaze, unsure of what he'd think of her after such an admission. Would he understand her fears or think she was a dramatic princess worried about nothing?

"I didn't realize—"

"I can be deep? A lot of people think I'm shallow." Her voice dropped lower. She didn't much care about other people's opinions, but having Andre believe she lacked substance would be a blow.

"I don't believe you're shallow, Monica. Spoiled, but not shallow."

The smile in his voice made her look up and prompted a smile to her face, as well.

"I can't deny I'm spoiled," she said.

They both laughed, which eased the tension in the room.

Monica clapped her hands together. "So, moving along. I'll encourage attendees to take selfies and use a hashtag I'll create for opening night, and I'll interview them for my IG stories."

"You have this all figured out."

"I told you, I know what I'm doing."

"Okay, here's my plan for opening night."

Andre went through his list of ideas, and for the next hour they worked on promotions leading up to the grand opening and the night of the opening. They worked flawlessly as a team, with the occasional joke tossed in.

By the end of the session, they had finalized the details for promoting the restaurant. Andre was satisfied, and Monica had a better understanding of his vision. He was sharp and organized. She didn't doubt for one minute that with him in charge, Midnight Lounge would be a success.

Andre gathered up the papers, some of which contained scribbled notes and drawings from their brainstormed ideas. With the meeting coming to an end, Monica felt a bit down. She searched her mind for a way to prolong their time together.

"You have lunch plans?" Andre asked.

Well, she didn't have to come up with an idea after all.

She cast a glance at him in surprise as her heart raced.

Chapter Eleven

He wanted to spend more time with her. Andre knew it was wrong but ignored the twinge of guilt that nicked his chest.

The conversation about the past, the reminiscing and joking around, and the business talk all reminded him of Monica's finer qualities. She had a great sense of humor and go-getter personality, all of which made her attractive. She was, in all honesty, the kind of woman he had—at one time—envisioned spending the rest of his life with.

His attraction to her was understandable because of their history, but he was getting married to Belinda. Maybe he and Monica could be friends. Friendly acquaintances, at least.

"I don't have plans," she answered. Caution laced her voice. "Are you inviting me to lunch?"

Andre closed the laptop and stood. "I am. It's on the company."

"Ooh, I'm going to eat well." She rose to her feet.

"Are you suggesting if I were the one responsible for paying, you wouldn't be eating well?"

She let out a laugh, and the sound boosted his spirits, as if he'd won the MVP trophy at a playoff game.

"I am not suggesting that at all," she said, eyes teasing.

"In that case, we can go to Notte. Never been there, but I heard the food is excellent."

"My brother, Ethan, loves that place. You'll love the seafood pasta."

While tucking the documents and laptop under his arm, Andre paused. "You remember I like seafood?"

"Yes." Her *Yes* sounded more like *Of course.*

The air stilled as they looked at each other.

"Can't wait to try it."

Monica walked ahead of him out the door, and his gaze dropped to the exposed skin of her back and the way the loose material of the romper draped over her hips and ass. His fingers itched to stroke her brown skin and go lower, but instead he lifted his gaze to fight the temptation.

"Give me a few minutes. I'ma go upstairs to drop these off, and then we can leave."

"I'll be waiting."

Her words made his chest tighten, a familiar sensation that used to plague him when they were together. He brushed off the feeling and took the elevator to the third floor. He dropped the items on the desk and made a quick call to the popular restaurant to reserve a table. Then he checked his appearance in the mirror on the wall, straightening his tie as he gazed at his reflection.

"What are you doing?" he asked himself quietly.

Setting himself up, because Monica was definitely a temptation. He could resist her, though. Had to. No way he'd allow himself to fall under her spell again. He took the stairs to the first floor, and she stood from the leather sofa in the waiting area.

"Ready?" he asked.

"Yes. I'm starving."

"I'll be back in about an hour and a half," he told the receptionists.

He held open the door and as they left the building and couldn't resist placing a hand at the small of Monica's back. Her skin was as soft as he remembered, and the tensing in her shoulders suggested she experienced the same thing he did. A charge of electricity. A flash of heat.

He dropped his hand immediately and watched her sashay ahead of him toward the parking lot in the back where his vehicle was parked.

On the drive to Notte, they continued their conversation about the lounge and tossed a few more ideas back and forth. The time passed quickly, and soon he was pulling into the parking lot. They entered the restaurant, already packed with a lunchtime crowd. Because he'd called ahead, they were immediately led to a booth, where they settled for lunch.

"I have another request," Monica said, leaning across the table like someone sharing a secret.

He could drown in the pools of her pretty brown eyes. Were her lips still petal soft? He could kiss her for hours and never get tired of her succulent mouth.

"What's your request?"

"No more talk about work."

"What do you want to talk about then?"

"Anything else. I haven't seen you in years. There should be plenty for us to discuss."

She was right, and he wanted to know everything about her.

"Deal."

After a few minutes, a server arrived with two glasses of water. A light-skinned woman with long braids wrapped around each other in a stylish twist atop her head, she told them the special, took their orders, and left them alone.

"How's your family?" Andre asked.

"Maxwell started his residency," Monica said.

"He's your youngest brother, right?"

Monica came from a big, blended family. When her mother and stepfather married, they had three children each. On her mother's side, an older brother and sister. On her stepfather's side, three boys. Then the couple had a child of their own.

She nodded. "He said the hours are kicking his butt, but I know he loves it. Being a doctor was what he talked about more than anything else growing up."

"And your parents?"

"They divorced a few years ago."

"No way."

"It was a surprise, but not really a surprise. Their relationship had been strained for a while, and then one day my mother asked my stepfather for a divorce, and he gave it to her."

"Just like that?"

"More or less. The crazy thing is, you'd barely know they were divorced. Papa Ben is always over at the house, and they act like best friends. The other day, he was having lower back pain, and I found them in the great room, my mother stretching out his lower back. The man is worth millions of dollars and can afford a trainer, but the only person who can satisfactorily stretch his back is my mother." She pursed her lips to express her skepticism.

Andre let out a knowing laugh. "Sounds like Papa Ben is trying to work his way back in there. Maybe they'll get back together."

"I don't know. It would be nice. My brother, Ethan is getting married."

She then filled him in on what her stepbrothers were

working on, and by the time she wrapped up the summary, the waitress returned with their drink orders and salads.

"What's the latest with your mom?" Monica asked, digging into her salad.

She knew all about how his mother had killed her boyfriend. One day she'd had enough, and she shot him dead. Despite her black eye, bruises, and busted lip, she was arrested and booked.

"Still working on her appeal."

His mother had been the one to encourage him to go to college, to 'make something of himself.' Once he got kicked out of UGA, he went to work full-time, finding employment as security at a nightclub. He studied his mother's case and made it his goal to set her free, sending all his extra cash to the lawyers. When he started working for Chambers Enterprises, he was able to set aside more money because of a higher salary and bonuses.

A hustler like his father, Andre figured out he could make more money faster if he invested, so he approached Nigel with the idea of putting capital in his businesses as a silent partner. He also did day trading and whatever he could to get a quick return. For every dollar Andre made, he set aside a dollar for his mother's attorney, determined to get her free. His one indulgence was the Escalade—the vehicle he'd wanted for years.

"How long has she been incarcerated?" Monica asked.

"Seventeen years now. I think she's losing hope, but I'm not. I'm never giving up."

He explained to her how the trial had been a farce. The judge had given his mother the maximum—life in prison—never taking into consideration the abuse she suffered under. Later, they discovered his son had died of an overdose, suspected of using drugs purchased from the same gang Andre's father had laundered money for. The judge should have recused himself, which had been the basis of their appeal, among other discrepancies during the trial.

The hands of justice moved slow, and she needed to be paid. The money his father had left all went to lawyers during his mother's trial. By the end, they'd run through their savings and lost the house they lived in.

Andre shoved lettuce around on his plate. "The attorneys said they're confident they can get a new trial, but she told me the best thing I could do is accept the situation. I hate to think I've lost my mother for good. Part of me accepts it, but it's not easy. If I don't accept she's in prison, I run the risk of flying to New York and putting a bullet in the judge's head."

"That's pretty harsh," Monica said quietly.

"That's how I feel. As far as I'm concerned, he took her life, so he should lose his." Talking to her was too easy. He was spilling his guts about dangerous fantasies.

"I'm sorry, Andre."

They ate in silence for a while.

"How long have you been engaged?" Monica asked in a casual tone.

He eyed her across the table. "You really want to talk about Belinda?"

"I'm a little curious. You don't have to tell me *everything*."

He set down his fork. "A'ight. We got engaged a few months back."

"When are you getting married?"

"Next year, spring."

Monica nodded and took a sip of her iced tea.

His mouth formed to ask about her relationship status, but he couldn't get the words out. He didn't want to know. Thinking about her with another man triggered a surge of jealousy and made his whole body rigid. He shouldn't have those feelings. He should feel nothing.

"Since you're already working for her father, one day you'll take over his business, I guess?"

"That's not my dream." Though he suspected it was Nigel's. The man had all but anointed him his next heir.

"What is your dream?"

"To open my own place, like I told you. The target demographic will be young Black professionals, aged twenty-one to thirty-five."

"Sounds like you've been doing research."

"I have. Matter fact, I already have a location."

Her eyes widened. "Where?"

He laughed. "Don't get excited. I don't have the money to buy the place yet, but it's in an up-and-coming area. I put together some sketches with ideas for the inside."

"Okay, but where?"

When he told her the part of town, Monica said, "I don't know that area very well. I guess it's really nice?"

"Not really. Like I said, up-and-coming. It has great potential because of condos going up nearby and a new shopping center minutes away. I could take you to see it, if you want."

The offer rolled off his tongue. Sharing his dreams and secrets with Monica had always been so easy. Whenever he had good news or wanted to share a goal, she was always the first person he called or texted. When they broke up, he sorely missed being able to reach out.

"I'd love to see it, if you have time."

He didn't. He should get back to the office to finish some paperwork and then go home to check his stock portfolio, but that's not what he said.

"Okay, Sunshine. Finish your meal, and I'll take you."

She froze, staring at him.

"What?"

"You called me Sunshine."

"Yeah," he said, surprised at how the endearment slipped past his lips without realizing it. "I did."

Their gazes locked across the table. He didn't know what she was thinking, but his mind's eye raced through the thousands of hours they had spent together—walking hand in hand on campus, making out in the back seat of his old Cadillac, the first time he looked into her eyes and whispered that he loved her.

To him, Monica had been his sunshine, his light, during the darkest years—the years after his mother's incarceration.

Chapter Twelve

Monica was vaguely familiar with this part of town. The cluster of defunct factories had been transformed into new, stylish apartments and condominiums with plenty of amenities. In the surrounding area, new places to shop—grocery stores and small shops where unique gifts could be purchased—were also cropping up. According to Andre, properties could be purchased cheap, but they needed a lot of work since the buildings had been abandoned for years.

The SUV bounced across a gravel road.

"Don't judge yet," Andre said.

"I'm not judging. I'm actually familiar with this area, a little bit at least."

He glanced at her, and she could see the excitement in his eyes.

They stopped at the back of a group of buildings in front of a two-story former warehouse with huge windows and a brick façade. Some of the windows are cracked, and the front door was boarded up.

"This is it."

Monica glanced around. There wasn't much in this part of the neighborhood.

Andre laughed. He seemed to be so much more at ease than in the past, she couldn't help but laugh too.

"What?" she asked.

"You should see your face."

"I mean, there's not much to see here. This part is completely underdeveloped. How did you find this building?"

"I subscribe to a commercial newsletter, and there was a whole article about this part of town, the availability of property, and the potential if someone had enough money to invest. You want to see the inside?"

"Sure. We're here. Let's do it."

Monica hopped down from the SUV and followed behind Andre. He took her to the side of the building to a boarded up window. The huge windows extended almost the full height of the wall. Grasping the board, he pulled it aside and revealed broken glass.

"Step over. Be careful."

He extended his hand, and she took it, holding on as she gingerly stepped over the low window ledge into the dusty, dank warehouse. Andre came in after her, and the board slid into place with a grating sound, sealing them inside where streams of light broke through the windows and minute cracks in the walls.

"I know it doesn't look like much," Andre began, his shoes crunching over broken glass and other debris littering the floor. "But this is the place where I'd like to open my lounge. I envision a chill spot for people looking to connect with other folks, grow their network, and have a good time outside of the usual club atmosphere. Back there, I want to set up a hookah bar. Now"—he faced her, forcing her to look in the same direction as him—"imagine, two bars, back to back, bisecting this whole space."

Monica nodded. "I can see it."

"On the right, lounge chairs for people to chill and sit, on the left, tables set up with curtains coming from the ceiling that they can close for privacy."

Monica swung to face him. "Ooh, great idea."

He continued, energized, as if he was a salesman and she a potential buyer. "We'll have a second floor, similar to the one at Midnight Lounge, where people can eat and enjoy a nice dinner while overlooking the entire lounge. Then picture a catwalk across the open space—"

"A catwalk?" Monica interrupted.

"Hold on, bear with me. A catwalk, where people can walk across, and then I'll have the offices set up at the front. From the offices I'll be able to see the parking lot, but also have a pretty good view of the entire floor."

Monica nodded, resting her hands on her hips "I like it."

Andre watched her with suspicious eyes. "Come on now. You serious?"

"Yes, I'm serious. It's a unique design, and if you're going to do something, go big and grand."

"Exactly what I was thinking."

Falling silent, he gazed off into the distance.

"When are you going to do all this?" She saw wonder on his face. "What?"

"You have a completely different reaction to someone else I showed this building to."

She wondered if the someone was Belinda. "Maybe because I have a brother whose deeply involved in real estate. Ethan is very wealthy, but he started with a place like this. Our stepfather loaned him the money to fix up a rundown building, and that's how he got his start."

"Yeah? That's cool. To answer your question, I can't work on this any time soon."

"You have to move on it. If there's interest in the area like you said, if you wait too long, you'll lose out. Someone else will get this space."

"I don't have the kind of money I need to purchase the property and then renovate, and I'm sure you see this place needs major work, so that ain't happening no time soon."

"You could get a loan."

"I could also win the lottery," he said sarcastically.

"Come on, Andre, you brought me here for a reason. You must be close."

"In my dreams," he muttered.

Her heart ached for him. "Do you already have a name?"

He grinned. "I do."

"I knew it! What's the name?" she asked, getting excited.

"NV Lounge. Spelled N-V."

"Ohmigosh, I love it! Go. Get. Your. Loan."

"It's not that easy, Monica."

"Nothing worth having comes easy. You have to work for it, *Andre*."

"Yeah, yeah."

"How much money do you need?"

He stroked the tuft of hair on his chin. "Hell, I don't know. I'm pulling together the information to write a business plan, but there are so many different kinds. The research alone is kicking my ass, and I'm screwed when it comes to actually writing the plan."

She giggled. Writing wasn't his strong suit. "Stop being cheap and pay someone to put it together for you. Outsource the tasks you don't want to do. It'll make your life so much easier."

"Says the woman who's a multi-millionaire and has a personal assistant."

"And that's how I know."

He chuckled. "Okay, you're right, and my cousin could probably help me. You might know a little something."

"A little?" She arched an eyebrow.

"Yeah. A little." He held his thumb and forefinger less than a quarter inch apart.

"Whatever." Laughing, she smacked down his hand.

He caught her by the wrist. "Why you always hitting?"

"I do not!"

"Some things never change."

His eyes scoured her face, and the air around them suddenly became restricted. His thumb stroked the inside of her wrist, over the interlocked hearts, and Monica felt each swipe all the way to her core.

Something scurried across her foot and she jumped, bumping into Andre's chest. "What the heck was that?"

A quick glance at the floor, and she saw a gray mouse disappear beneath a pile of beams.

"Ew! A mouse." She shivered and turned her face into his chest.

His chest trembled with laughter. "It's not the end of the world."

She gazed up at him. "Did the mouse run across your foot? No. That was disgusting."

"I better get you out of here, then."

Instead of moving, the hand not holding her wrist slipped to her back.

"Damn, you're so soft," Andre whispered, spreading his fingers over her skin.

Monica pulled back, not because she didn't want his touch but because she recognized the danger ahead. The fingers around her wrist held her fast, and his arm tightened around her, dropping low on her back, right above her ass. She held her breath.

His other hand gently ran up and down her bare arm. "Some things really never change," he said, keeping his voice low.

The mouse, the dusty interior of the warehouse—everything was forgotten as his head lowered to hers. She hadn't realized how much she wanted him to kiss her until their lips touched. The kiss was explosive, feverish. Her lips trembled beneath his, and her hand reached up to cup his cheek.

The heat from the sun was no match for the heat radiating around them, engulfing them in scorching hunger. She flung her arms around his neck and explored his body—his broad shoulders, the muscular biceps of his arms, his chest and face, his head. She touched him everywhere, locked into a deep, frantic kiss.

She needed him. Ached for him. Nothing else mattered in that moment but having more of Andre. His kisses covered her temple, her cheeks, all the way down to the base of her neck. Her head tipped back so he could explore her throat, his breath coming in harsh spurts as he sucked and kissed her sensitive skin.

"Andre," she moaned, voice thick and pleading.

The next thing she knew, her feet were off the ground, and her legs wrapped around his waist. He hadn't lifted her so much as she had climbed him. Long-fingered hands held her thighs in a possessive grip, his right hand sliding beneath the opening of her romper to cup her left butt cheek. With her arms locked around Andre's neck, she clung to him and enjoy every caress and kiss. She could barely breath, suffocating with unbridled desire as she grinded her hips against him for relief.

Then, out of nowhere, and interruption. Disoriented by

lust, she didn't understand what was happening at first, but they were pressed so closely together the phone in his pocket vibrated against her inner thigh. Andre groaned and tore his mouth from hers, and Monica took two deep breaths to bring her breathing under control.

She swallowed hard, her body still throbbing from the pleasure of feeling him against her, his hand roaming freely over her skin in decadent caresses.

She lowered to her feet, and he lifted the phone from his pocket. His face fell, and he turned sideways and answered.

"Hello?" Andre swiped a hand across his mouth. "What are you doing there?" Pause. "No, I'm at lunch... with a client." His gaze met hers, and she knew right away he was talking to Belinda.

She started for the broken window. Andre grabbed her arm as he continued talking, but she couldn't understand a word he said. She felt like someone under water and needed to reach the surface so she could breathe.

She shook off his hand and hurried across the cement floor littered with debris on its surface. She tried to drag aside the board, but it was heavy, and she couldn't get any leverage from the inside.

Andre came up beside her, still talking. "I didn't know you were going to come by the office," he said.

She didn't want to hear another word. She couldn't look at him, her heart racing out of control, her face burning in shame.

With one hand, he shoved the board and slipped his fingers to the outside. Getting a good grip on the edge, he yanked the wood covering aside.

Monica didn't look at him as she stepped outside and hurried away.

Chapter Thirteen

What the hell is wrong with me? Monica berated herself, standing beside the passenger door of the Escalade.

She couldn't believe she had done that. She didn't kiss other women's fiancés.

Footsteps on the gravel made her to turn and see Andre coming toward her, no longer on the phone. Her heart beat against her chest as she waited to hear what he had to say.

He stopped several feet away. "What happened in there..."

"Shouldn't have happened," she finished for him.

"No, it shouldn't have."

"Was that her on the phone?"

"Yes."

"What did you say?"

"You heard what I said. We didn't talk much. I told her I would come to the office when I finished with my lunch meeting."

They both fell silent, neither looking at the other. Too

dangerous. Desire continued to pulse between them, and she was afraid of what she would do. She wanted the heat of his touch and rush of his lips against hers, no matter how wrong it was.

"I can't believe I did that." He shook his head in disgust.

"We spent several hours together, and obviously old feelings resurfaced. That's it. Nothing more."

"Nothing more? If the phone hadn't rung, there's a very good possibility I would have fucked you against the closest hard surface."

Her insides quivered at the rawness of his words.

"I've been thinking about you a lot, and I don't like it," he continued. "I don't fucking cheat, Monica. That's not who I am."

"You think that's who I am?" she demanded.

"Fuck, fuck, fuck!" He paced away from her, shoulders rigid with tension. He glared at her from ten feet away. "Why did you...?"

The question trailed away on his lips, but she finished the sentence in her head because it was the same question she'd silently asked him a million times. Why did you come back into my life?

Suddenly chilled in the warm spring air, she wrapped her arms around herself. "If you're done with the self-flagellation, could you take me back to the office now? Please."

"Monica—"

"What do you want me to say! You're engaged. So let's cut the bullshit and speak honestly. We're both horny for the past but the kiss was a mistake. Call it nostalgia, call it whatever you want, but it's best if we both pretend this didn't happen. The kiss didn't happen."

"Just like that? It didn't happen." His nostrils flared as he became more furious at her words.

"You're engaged. That's how it has to be, isn't it?" She asked the question, knowing the correct answer yet secretly hoping for a different outcome.

"And what about you. You seeing anyone? You have a man?"

"Nothing serious," Monica muttered.

"I don't believe you. There's gotta be someone."

"Yes, I date. I have a need for companionship like everyone else on the planet!" she snapped.

Andre came closer, and she backed up, careful not to touch the hot metal exterior of the SUV. He stared into her eyes.

"I'm jealous, and I have no right to be. The thought of anyone else touching you, kissing you, fucking you is driving me out of my mind. In case it wasn't clear back there, *I* want to be the one to do those things. So that makes me a piece of shit, don't it? Because I shouldn't be thinking about you in that way. I shouldn't be thinking about how I want to make you give up every other man in your life."

The heat of his words chased away the chill that had consumed her, and to her horror acknowledge she *would* give up every other lover for a chance to be with Andre again. She'd done it in college. Ecstatic for the freedom to come and go as she pleased for the first time in her life, she dated different men until she met Andre. She gave them all up for him and would willingly do it again. All he had to do was say the word, and she'd do what he told her to.

In his bed, she became a goddess, and the fantasy of being pinned beneath him had lived rent-free in her head since last week when he surprised her by entering the board room. She hated the thought of *him* being touched and kissed and loved on by someone else. He had been hers first and she'd lost him, and she hated that Belinda would have him forever.

Andre took several steps back, indicating a clear need to

create distance and dispel the current of attraction that remained a constant between them.

"You're right. This didn't happen." He took a deep breath and gazed at the warehouse behind her.

She understood what he was thinking. He had too much to lose. His fiancée. His standing with her father. His livelihood. A chance to help his mother. Getting involved with Monica meant losing everything he'd worked for over the years. He would be a fool to risk all of that for her.

"This didn't happen," she repeated in agreement.

She was a performer. She performed every day on social media and could pretend he hadn't turned her world upside down in a matter of days.

Andre disengaged the locks with the remote and opened the passenger door. Monica climbed in and watched him walk to the other side of the vehicle.

When he entered on the driver side, she snapped her seatbelt closed and angled her knees away from him. Gazing out the window, she pressed against the door the same way she did the first time she climbed into his vehicle.

They rode back to Chambers Enterprises in complete silence.

"Hey, are you okay?" Daisy asked. She sat on the loveseat at the foot of Monica's bed, watching her pace back and forth with her arms crossed.

"No, I'm not okay."

"What can I do to help?"

She stopped pacing and with great effort stifled the urge to scream. "Nothing."

"You're so upset, though. There must be something I can do."

Monica rested her hands on her hips. "Do you know how to make me stop feeling like a crazy person?"

"I don't, but I'm a good listener. Sit." She pulled Monica onto the loveseat and then got a chair from by the window. She sat in the chair and crossed one leg over the other. "Pretend I'm your therapist."

Monica laughed.

"I'm serious. Tell me whatever is on your mind." She patiently waited.

Realizing she was serious, Monica took a deep breath and released it slowly. "I'm upset about Andre."

"Did something happen at the meeting? What did he do?"

"What did *we* do."

Daisy's eyes widened.

"No, we didn't have sex, but..." Her voice dropped. "We might have if his phone didn't ring."

"Start from the beginning."

Haltingly at first, Monica explained about the meeting, lunch at Notte, the visit to the warehouse, and the ensuing heated kiss.

Daisy leaned forward, hanging on her every word. When Monica finished, she straightened in the chair. "Wow. The two of you clearly still have chemistry."

"He's involved with someone, though. Seriously involved," Monica pointed out.

"But if he has feelings for you, the heart wants what the heart wants."

"I don't know." Monica gnawed her thumbnail.

"What do you like about him? What makes him irresistible after all this time?"

She didn't answer right away. Then she whispered, "Every-thing." The answer stripped her so bare, her chest felt as if it caved in from longing. "The way he walks. The way he talks. The way he looks at me. His sense of humor." She rubbed a hand across her forehead. "The memories from back in college don't help."

"The memories?" Daisy prompted.

"Of how things used to be between us. Hot. He's..." She let the sentence fade away, her cheeks flaming with heat and her body throbbed with renewed hunger.

"Good in bed," Daisy finished for her.

Monica nodded. "Unmatched."

"Wow."

"He's the only man I've been monogamous with," she admitted.

He consumed me. He tapped spots no one else has ever touched.

"Sounds like you were dick-whipped."

"I was definitely dick-whipped."

They both laughed.

"How do you think he feels?" Daisy asked.

"Guilty about the kiss and his attraction to me. Like I said, we agreed to pretend as if nothing happened."

"Can you do that?"

"I'm going to do my best."

They both fell silent.

Daisy perked up. "You know what you need?"

"What?"

"A chocolate smoothie."

Monica laughed. "How do you always know what I need before I do?"

"ESP. Come on, let's go. You relax while I drive." Daisy popped up from the chair, and they exited the bedroom.

They climbed into the Cayenne, and Daisy took the wheel. Halfway to the smoothie shop, she remarked, "This car drives so smooth."

"It does. I love my baby," Monica said. She propped her bare feet on the dashboard and gazed out the window.

What was Andre doing now? Was he thinking about her as much as she was thinking about him?

"It's out of my budget, but one of these days, I'm getting one," Daisy continued.

"That means you'll leave me," Monica wailed.

"I'll never leave you." Daisy grinned and squeezed her hand.

"Good. Cause I don't know what I'd do without you."

They pulled into the drive-thru of the smoothie shop and ordered two large chocolate smoothies.

"I'm hooked on these now too," Daisy said, taking a long sip and then setting her smoothie in the cup holder.

"I'm a bad influence."

"Yes, you are."

Monica pulled out her camera. "We should take a picture."

"Nooo."

"Yes, come on." She leaned toward Daisy, and Daisy leaned toward her. "Hold up your smoothie like me."

Daisy did as she asked, laughing. "We're practically twins."

"That's what we'll say instead of cheese. On the count of three—one, two, three..."

"Twins!" they both said, and Monica snapped the photo.

Afterward, Daisy pulled out of the lot and headed back to the house.

Monica gazed at her. In a short time, she'd become more than an assistant. She considered her a trusted companion and friend. Their relationship had blossomed in an unexpected way, and thanks to Daisy, she was no longer in a bad mood.

"I'm so glad you're in my life," she said.

Daisy smiled at her. "Me too."

Chapter Fourteen

Andre walked into the shower stall and turned the water to a cold temperature. He needed Monica out of his head and needed to forget how she felt like in his arms—the texture of her skin, the scent of her perfume. Almost impossible when his body still throbbed hours later.

Worse, he didn't regret the stolen moments with her. Their conversations energized him, and the kissing and touching had felt right.

After they returned to the office, she thanked him for lunch as if nothing else had occurred during the more time they spent together. Then she climbed into her Porsche Cayenne and left the lot. Fortunately for him, Belinda had already left, so he shut the office door—one of the rare occasions he did—so as not to be bothered by anyone. He left an hour later because he couldn't concentrate and had been at home trading until Belinda came over in the evening.

He placed a hand on his sensitive penis. He should be thinking about the woman in the other room, but Monica was the reason he was as rigid as a steel pole. Sex with Belinda was good, and for the most part he was satisfied, but there were things she wouldn't do in bed and no amount of coaxing changed her mind. He had resigned himself to do without because they were compatible in other ways, but Monica was an uninhibited lover, willing to experiment in, and out, of bed.

He'd fucked her in the parking lot of the football stadium, bent over the hood of his Cadillac as she moaned her pleasure into the cold metal hood of the car. He'd taken her against the outside wall of a local bar, minutes after the place closed for the night and students had been forced to go home. He'd lost track of how many times they'd made love in his bed and hers, their bodies moving in sync, their cries of passion mingling together like a raunchy duet.

Two times. He'd seen her two times and was already second-guessing his future with the woman he intended to marry. She should wear a goddamn sign that said *Danger,* or better yet, *Here comes trouble.*

Hand on the wall, Andre stroked his soapy dick, head bent as the water pummeled his back. He moaned at a low level, a combined sound of agony and disgust at what he'd been reduced to doing because he couldn't have what he wanted.

He imagined thrusting inside her, and memories from the past bombarded him to aid in the fantasy. Her long legs wrapped around his hips. Her pleading pants begging him to go harder and deeper. Then he remembered what it was like to have her lips locked around his dick, hearing her moan as she relaxed her jaw to take him deeper.

The hand on the wall curled into a ball as he stroked faster. Then the shower door popped open, and his head snapped up guiltily. *Shit.* He was so close.

Belinda stepped naked into the shower with him, hair piled on top of her head, eyes watching him flirtatiously.

"Is that for me?" she asked, glancing down at his erection.

A jagged laugh scraped his throat on the way up. Guilt kept him from lying, so he didn't directly answer the question. She slipped her arms around his waist.

"Need some help?" she asked with raised eyebrows, voice hopeful.

Andre extricated himself from her arms without—he hoped —making it obvious he didn't want to be touched right then. She wouldn't understand. He barely understood himself.

"I'm bushed. I don't have the energy," he said, letting the water rinse the soap off his body.

She eyed his erection. "You sure?"

He laughed again to play off the irony of having an erection but not wanting to have sex. "I'm sure."

Without another word, he stepped out of the shower and grabbed a towel. After quickly rubbing his skin dry, he wrapped it around his waist and exited the bathroom.

Much later, he lay awake in bed with Belinda beside him. She hadn't said a word about him abandoning her in the bathroom, but he was certain it would come up again. That's the way she operated. She didn't always say what was on her mind in the moment, but later she'd broach the topic when he least expected and catch him off guard.

He listened to her breathing next to him, head resting on one of the satin pillowcases she kept at his place. After a while, he eased off the bed and went over to the dresser. He rolled a blunt and after casting another quick glance at Belinda's sleeping form, pushed aside the vertical blinds and opened the sliding glass door as quietly as he could. He walked onto the balcony and rested his forearms on the metal railing, smoking while he observed his environment.

The neighborhood was quiet, most of the windows dark, a few lit up with the curtains closed. Different-sized brick buildings filled the neighborhood—some multiple stories high holding two or four apartments on each floor. Others were like his, two stories but one apartment. There were four apartments in his building, but he was lucky to have gotten an end unit. The renter next to him traveled a lot and when he was home was so quiet, at times Andre forgot he had a neighbor.

At the sound of the glass door sliding behind him, his heart sank. He wanted—*needed*—time alone to think.

Glancing over his shoulder, he saw Belinda standing in the doorway in a white, see-through, baby doll nightie. She might as well have been wearing an oversized potato sack for all the interest his dick had in her.

"Did I wake you?" he asked.

She shook her head, tousled hair shaking with the movement. "Are you okay?" she asked.

He didn't deserve her concern. He straightened from the railing, careful to hold the blunt away from her so the scent wouldn't waft in her direction. She didn't like the smell of weed.

"Yeah, of course."

"You seem distracted lately, and now you're out here in the middle of the night instead of in bed with me."

He took a draw on the joint and blew smoke out the corner of his mouth, away from her. "I have a lot on my mind."

"Anything I can help with?"

"No. I want everything to go well with the restaurant, that's all." A partial truth. He did want a good return on his investment.

"Baby, I told you about your perfectionist attitude. It's unrealistic." She stepped out and rubbed a soothing hand up and down his arm. "Everything will be fine."

"You're right."

She graced him with a soft smile.

"Go to bed. I'll be in, in a minute." He kissed her cheek because she would not allow him to kiss her lips right now.

"Hurry up. I love you." She gazed up at him, still smiling. The moment stretched between them, and her smile wavered. With a jolt, Andre realized he hadn't said the words back to her.

"I love you too." The words were hard to come by and left his mouth feeling chalky and dry.

The moment became awkward because they both knew he'd taken too long to repeat the words that should flow easily and automatically from his lips.

Her face brightened with a fake smile.

"Don't take too long," she whispered. She went back inside and closed the door.

Andre shut his eyes. He had to get Monica out of his head and out of his life.

Immediately.

* * *

"What are you doing? Spring cleaning?" Maxwell asked.

Monica positioned her phone on a stand inside her walk-in closet in such a way her brother could see her as she browsed through the clothes. Designed in white throughout, the space wasn't as large as she would like, but it was big enough to function as a dressing room and stuffed with enough items to fill a small boutique.

A built-in dresser hid scarves, folded T-shirts, and casual clothing. Built-in shelves held a partial collection of her shoes, with the overflow in one of the guest bedroom closets. Most of her clothes hung on hangers behind glass doors, and the lesser used items—such as certain handbags—were stored at the top of the closet on open shelves only accessible via a small step ladder in the corner.

"I'm looking for something for Daisy to wear. I'm taking her to the opening of the lounge with me," Monica explained.

"You've never taken her out before. What prompted you to do that?" Maxwell covered a yawn with his hand.

At the moment, he was lying on a cot at the hospital. He should be trying to sleep, but when she called earlier to check on him, he put off sleeping so they could catch up.

Since he was the youngest of her siblings, she loved to tease him, calling him the baby which he abhorred. A combination of his Black and Mexican parents, he was brown-skinned with loosely curled hair which currently spiked in different directions from combing his fingers through it.

"She doesn't go out, and I decided to take her with me so she could get out and socialize a little bit."

"And by socialize, you mean find a man?"

"You're so smart. I guess that's why you're going to be a doctor."

Maxwell smiled. "The two of you aren't the same size. She's about two sizes bigger than you," he pointed out.

"How do you know what size she is? Have you been checking out my assistant, little brother?"

He laughed. "I'm not blind."

"Mhmm." Maxwell was a woman magnet and took advantage of his attraction to the opposite sex. "I have a few things she can wear, but if I don't find anything in my closet, I'm taking her shopping." Monica lifted a floor length dress off its hanger. "Not this," she said, and immediately replaced it.

"That's nice of you. I'm sure she'll appreciate it."

"She deserves it, you know? She works really hard, and I want to do something nice for her. Plus she listens to me whine and complain all the time, including today."

"What happened today?"

"Oh, nothing important." She didn't want to discuss her conflicted feelings about Andre with her brother. Besides, the chat with Daisy helped a lot. "A new outfit and going out with me isn't much, but she could meet someone."

"That's how you lost your last assistant."

"I know," Monica groaned. "Speaking of meeting someone, what about you?"

"You're kidding, right? I don't have time to date. My life is work and sleep. Sometimes I eat."

"Sounds awful."

"It could be, but this is what I want to do, so I'm going to suck it up." He yawned again. "I hate to do this, but I need catch some Z's."

Monica picked up the phone. "Okay, get your rest. Proud of you."

"Thanks. Proud of you too. You're doing your thing. Tah-tah," he said with a grin and threw up the peace sign.

Monica repeated the sign at him. "Tah-tah, baby brother."

After they hung up, the smile fell away from her face, and she dropped her butt to the ottoman covered in faux white fur. He wouldn't be proud if he knew she'd kissed someone else's fiancé today. Monica buried her face in her hands.

You'll be fine, she thought.

The lounge opened in three weeks, which meant she had three weeks to recuperate and get over her feelings for Andre. If she survived opening night, she'd never have to see his handsome face again.

Chapter Fifteen

Andre strolled through Midnight Lounge, stopping every now and then to check on patrons, making sure the food satisfied their palates and the drinks were strong enough to give the buzz they craved after a long day's work.

The place was packed, but there weren't many people on the dance floor. Jazmine Sullivan wafted through the speakers while two couples danced and one guy danced by himself, cradling his drink to his chest, eyes closed. Poor bastard must have had a hard week.

Most everyone seemed satisfied and in a good mood. A group of sorority sisters crowded around a table drinking colorful drinks. Two men and a woman sat at another table eating heavy hors d'oeuvres and laughing uproariously.

Near the bar, a woman in a business suit was hemmed in between two stools by a stocky brother. The young woman held a drink, but her body language spoke volumes. She leaned away from the man towering over her, like a scared rabbit about to dart away. Some men couldn't read signals—or did but completely ignored them.

Andre approached and dropped a heavy hand on the man's shoulder. "Hey, how you are you two doing tonight?"

"Doing great," the man answered.

"Drinks okay?"

"Perfect. This place gonna be my new spot."

Andre turned his attention to the young woman. "How about you? You doing okay tonight?"

"Fine," she said in a meek voice.

"Do you have a few minutes? I want to show you something we have especially for the ladies tonight."

She perked up. "Sure, I don't mind."

"Excuse us," Andre said, edging the man out of the way and leading the woman in the direction he wanted with a hand at her upper back.

He led her to the handrail near the stage. "Was that guy bothering you?"

She let out a heavy breath. "I don't want to get anyone in trouble."

"You won't. I only want to know if I should keep an eye on him."

She hesitated, then said, "He was a little aggressive, but I couldn't figure out how to politely get away."

"I peeped that." He pulled a card from his inside jacket pocket. "Listen, we want all our guests to be comfortable here. Take this. See here, it lists several codes you can use if you need assistance. For instance, you tell the bartender or one of the servers you'd like to order a Beachy Bomb, and they'll know you need someone to escort you to your car. Our people are real discreet and won't make a scene. If you lose this, go into the ladies bathroom where all the codes are also posted."

A relieved expression came over her face, and she took the card. "Thank you so much."

"You by yourself?"

"Two of my girlfriends are supposed to meet me tonight, but they're running late."

"Tell you what, go up to our VIP section, and call your girlfriends and let them know where you're sitting. I'll make sure that guy doesn't bother you again."

He'd made up a VIP section, but the more he thought about it, the more he realized it could be a financial coup for them. He'd text the idea to Nigel tomorrow.

"What was your name again?" the woman asked.

"Andre. I'm one of the owners."

"Nice to meet you Andre. Thank you."

She extended her hand, and her expression went from relief and appreciation to interest. "Tiffany," she said.

"Nice to meet you, Tiffany." They briefly shook hands.

When he tried to take back his hand, she held on. "Perhaps you should keep me company in case the guy from the bar comes back."

He let out a soft laugh and eased his hand from hers. "As one of the owners, I have a lot to take care of. Don't worry, though, he won't bother you again. I'll ask security to keep an eye on him."

"I feel safe already," she cooed.

"You have a good night, Tiffany."

"Thank you, Andre."

As she climbed the stairs, Andre walked over to Juan, a member of the security staff dressed in a black T-shirt and black pants. The Nicaraguan was about five-ten with a muscular build and a constant frown on his face.

"Juan, do me a favor. Keep an eye on the guy over there in the blue and white striped tie. He hasn't actually done anything yet, but I have a hunch we might have to ban him from the bar. He's a little aggressive."

"Sure thing, boss. I'll keep an eye on him."

Andre tapped Juan's shoulder in thanks and walked away.

Boss. He liked the sound of the word. One day he'd really be a boss, with his own place, like his father used to have. Except his establishment would be legit and not a front for laundering drug money.

Returning to the bar, he caught the bartender's attention. "Vodka with a twist of lemon," he said, and the bartender acknowledged the order with a nod.

Belinda hadn't shown up yet, but he expected her to. She was with her girlfriends doing something or other, and for the moment, he preferred that she wasn't there. Whenever she arrived, she'd demand his attention, and right now he needed to concentrate on the restaurant.

His eyes traveled over the room and snagged on the sight of Monica coming toward him. His insides seized at the vision she made strutting through the restaurant. If he didn't know better, he'd swear patrons stepped out of the way as she crossed the floor like a runway model. She sure knew how to make an entrance.

She wore a champagne-colored silk dress with a split reaching high on her left thigh. With every step she took, her hips swung from side to side, and the dress shimmered and waved from the sensual movement of her body in high heels. Spaghetti straps lay on her smooth shoulders, and large brass-colored earrings in her ears rocked as she spoke animatedly with the man beside her. More makeup tonight—dark color on her lips, dramatic black encircling eyes, and a reddish bronze color highlighting her cheeks.

Males and females followed her movement across the floor.

She waved, smiled, and nodded to several people, acknowledging them the way a superstar did raving fans.

He was so taken with her appearance, he was abruptly rocked when the man beside her slipped an arm around her waist. Andre stiffened, eyes latching onto the movement, and examined the imposter. Powder-blue shirt and black slacks, with a small gold hoop in one earlobe. Full beard, caramel-toned skin, and a slick, annoying smile as he whispered something to Monica.

She flashed a smile when she saw Andre, but he could not summon a reciprocal expression. His tense body became more tense when they stopped a few feet away. The man beside her aggravated the hell out of him by not removing his hand from around her waist.

Who the hell was he?

"We're here. The party can begin," she said, bright smile on her face. Now that they were closer, he could see the color on her lips was a deep, dark chocolate. They appeared moist and soft, and he had the overwhelming urge to lock lips with her again.

They had agreed to act as if the kiss didn't happen, and she was doing an excellent job of acting. Though her performance grated on his nerves, it prompted him to follow her lead.

"You brought a friend," Andre said.

"Friends. This is Donald. Donald, meet Andre. This is my assistant, Daisy." She stepped aside so he could see the woman he hadn't noticed walking behind her the entire time.

"Nice to meet you," Daisy said.

She was brown-skinned with friendly eyes and wore a strapless red dress with a high-low hemline, which she paired with three-inch heels and small earrings in her ears.

"Where's our table?" Monica asked.

The bartender placed the previously ordered vodka and

lemon on the bar, and Andre swept it up. He took a huge swallow. "This way."

He marched to a table with a *Reserved* sign on the surface. "This is you," he said.

"Perfect location. We can see the DJ and the dancefloor," Monica remarked.

"This *is* nice," the guy said.

His comment prompted Andre to speak up. "And who are you?"

Monica answered. "I told you, his name is Donald. He's a friend of mine."

A friend of mine. Not, my boyfriend or my fiancé.

He wanted to know if they were serious, but it was hard to tell with Monica. She'd been a wild child, happy to get away from her parents and brothers. She'd partied and enjoyed casual sex, never taking herself or relationships too seriously. Yet she'd become serious with Andre, embracing monogamy and leaving the other men behind.

So who was Donald to her? A casual lover or someone more serious? Andre hadn't seen him in any of the pictures on her Instagram page, so maybe they weren't serious, and at the warehouse she'd denied having a boyfriend.

Thoughts he shouldn't have invaded his mind. Thoughts of sliding her dress higher and kissing the inside of her thighs. He knew the sound of her arousal—a sound branded in his brain since the first night they made love. Monica had been generous and giving in bed, vulnerable and open with him.

He shoved away the sensual fantasy. The last thing he needed was to get a hard-on in the middle of the lounge.

"I assigned one server to you all night. Her name is Jenny. She knows to bring you anything you want. I'd love to stick around and chat, but I have a million things to do."

"That's understandable," Donald said.

Andre glanced at him, tempted to choke him out. Why the fuck was he talking? Andre was talking to Monica, not him, yet he inserted himself into the conversation.

"I'm parched. I hope Jenny comes by soon," Monica said.

"I'll make sure she does and takes care of you guys. I need to make my rounds. Let me know if you need anything."

"I will," she said.

Her gaze lingered on him, their eyes connecting in a secret message of forbidden desire.

A tingle scurried up his spine before he turned and walked away.

Chapter Sixteen

Standing on the outskirts of the venue, Monica held up her phone and took a selfie with a follower. They stood cheek to cheek, posing with puckered lips for the camera.

After she took the shot, her fan said, "Ohmigosh, thank you, Monica. Are you going to post this one?"

"Already done." Monica turned her phone so the other woman could see the screen.

She squealed and then pulled Monica into a quick but tight hug. "Thank you."

Monica flashed the peace sign, and they both said "Tah-tah, bitch" at the same time. The woman then scurried away to her table.

Despite being an influencer, she sometimes couldn't believe she had fans—over three million of them—who liked her posts, chatted with her in the comments, and shared her videos with their friends. They wanted to be *her* friend. They imitated her actions and obsessed over her product choices. The entire idea was overwhelming and exhilarating at the same time.

"You're *very* popular." Andre's deliciously gruff voice came from behind her, and unwelcome pinpricks of heat popped onto her arms.

She glanced over her shoulder. His eyes locked on her back, her skin exposed by the dangerously low dip in the dress. He took a step forward to stand on her left side, and she did a quick assessment of him from head to toe. Fresh haircut. Smelled good, as usual. Pure, raw sex appeal in a tempting brown package.

"Which is why your company hired me."

"So, what's the deal with Donald?" Andre asked casually.

"What do you mean?"

"He your boyfriend?"

Monica let out a short laugh. "He's a friend."

"You don't have male friends."

"Actually, I do, thank you very much."

"Since when?" He watched her sideways.

"Since forever."

"I'm not talking about friends with benefits," he said, dropping his voice lower.

She placed a hand on her hip. "I have platonic male friends, Andre."

"So you're not fucking him?"

The blunt question shocked her. "Excuse me?"

"You heard me."

"What business is it of yours? You have a fiancée."

His steady gaze didn't alter. "Just tell me if you're fucking him. It's a simple yes or no answer."

Jealousy lurked beneath the words. She couldn't forget their kiss from several weeks ago, and perhaps he couldn't either.

"Why do you want to know?" she asked.

"Because I want to."

"Green is an interesting color on you," she remarked.

His eyes narrowed. "I'm not jealous, if that's what you're implying."

"Are you sure?"

He laughed softly, narrowing his eyes more than usual. "You'll never change, will you?"

"What do you mean?"

"Still sassy. Still full of shit."

A peal of laughter escaped her throat. "I'll take that as a compliment."

"It was a compliment. You're one of a kind."

His eyes dipped to her chest and her breasts tightened. Breathing became difficult. How could she continue to act as if nothing happened when he examined her as if he wanted to tear off her clothes?

This is what Andre did to her, had always done to her. A simple compliment left her breathless, nipples tight. She put up a good front, but no one made her body ache the way simply standing next to him—not even touching—did.

"I'm not."

"Not what?"

"Sleeping with him. Not that it's any of your business. Satisfied?"

"Okay. So there's someone else, because we both know you have an appetite. Unless you've turned over a new leaf and become celibate."

Monica snorted at the ridiculous of his statement.

"You still have the same appetite—the same needs?" The bridges of his nose flared.

"You're getting dangerously close to being inappropriate. Matter of fact, I'd say you've crossed the line. We both know you have no business asking me that."

"You're right, I don't. Whoever he is, I know it's not serious because he's not on your Instagram feed."

"You went to my Instagram feed?"

"For work-related reasons."

"Uh-huh. Is that all, Andre?" She stepped closer. "Did you see the pictures of me in my orange bikini on St. John?"

"Don't start nothing you can't finish."

"I'm not the one who can't finish. You have a situation, don't you? Stop stalking my page and worrying about what I'm doing and with who."

"Stalking?"

"Yes, stalking. I'm calling it like I see it."

"*Heyyy!*"

At the exact moment she heard the high-pitched voice, a shorter, more voluptuous woman pushed her way between them. Belinda. She wore a tight red dress that clung to her breasts and ample behind. She flung her arms around Andre's neck and pulled him down for a loud kiss.

Tilting back her head, she said. "Hi, baby. Sorry I'm late."

Andre seemed significantly less enthusiastic than she did. Stiffly but gently, he removed her arms from around his neck.

"You were supposed to call before you came," he said.

"I wanted to surprise you. Who's this?" She turned her attention to Monica.

"You know who she is."

"Do I?" Belinda asked with obvious fake confusion. Her gaze flicked over Monica's outfit.

"Monica Connor," Andre said.

"Oh right, I remember you said something about her. Nice to meet you. You're the Instagram girl, right?"

Monica glanced at Andre, but his expressionless face gave nothing away. "Yes, I'm an influencer, and I'm helping promote the lounge. Your father hired me. Let me guess, you're Belinda?"

"Has Andre talked about me?" Obviously pleased at the idea, she cast a flirtatious smile from the corner of her eye at Andre.

"No. I just guessed," Monica said, voice dripping with honey.

Belinda's smile faltered, and guilt replaced Monica's moment of feeling good at taking her down a peg.

Andre cleared his throat. "It was good talking to you, Monica. You and your guests have enough to drink and eat?"

"I know what to do to get what I need. You go ahead and attend to your girlfriend."

"Fiancée," Belinda corrected.

"My bad. Talk to you later, Andre."

Then Monica walked away from them.

* * *

"Huh?"

Andre whipped his head from the second floor view where he observed the patrons milling around and enjoying themselves. Including Monica, who at the moment was playfully twerking at her table with Daisy and another woman. With the lights dimmed in the office, no one could tell he watched the three women laugh hysterically as they vied for Donald's attention, who clearly enjoyed himself dancing with each woman in turn.

Belinda stood in the middle of the office with her hands on her hips, an annoyed expression on her face.

"I said, when are you coming back downstairs?"

"Can't right now. I'm busy."

"Busy doing what? You were just standing there."

Andre bit back a sharp retort and shuffled papers on his desk. "I wasn't just standing here. I was surveying the floor, making sure things are running smoothly. Why did you pretend you didn't know who Monica was?"

"Why was she all up in your face?" Belinda countered.

"She wasn't all up in my face," Andre mumbled, annoyed.

She repositioned her arms across her chest. "I hate when you get like this."

"Like what?"

"Noncommittal. Why did I bother to come? You're not paying any attention to me."

"*I'm working.*" Andre kept his voice even.

"Yeah, right." Belinda tapped her right foot. "What do you think I'm doing?"

"I don't know, but I know my father gave you this position and you seem more interested in seeing what's going on down there than actually doing the job."

His control snapped, and Andre marched over to where Belinda stood. Her arms fell away, and her eyes widened as she took a few steps back. True enough Nigel had given him opportunities others might not because of his criminal background, but he worked hard and did a damn good job.

"I *earned* this spot. Don't you ever say no shit like that to me again."

Silence filled the room as he silently raged and she swallowed, shamefaced.

"I'm sorry. I didn't mean it," Belinda said in a small voice.

She appeared to be genuinely contrite, but he didn't care.

"You need to go." He gave her his back and returned to his spot behind the desk. Picking up a slip of paper, he pretended to read it.

"I'm sorry. Andre!"

"Bye, Belinda," he said, without looking at her.

"Not until you say you forgive me."

He continued to pretend to be preoccupied with the writing on the paper.

She came behind the desk. "I just want your attention. You've been so distracted lately, and tonight it's worse."

"It's opening night of the restaurant," he pointed out.

She nodded. "I know, and I understand. I'm being selfish and silly. You have a lot on your plate."

"I do, and I could really use your support, instead of whatever you have going on."

She readily nodded her agreement and came closer. Wrapping her arms around his waist, she leaned her body into him. "I love you so much, sometimes I feel insecure."

Guilt twisted like a corkscrew in his chest. "You're a beautiful woman. You shouldn't feel insecure."

Belinda batted her eyes and smiled. She pulled his face down to hers and gave him a warm, soft kiss.

"I'll be good, and I'll leave you alone so you can get your work done. Promise me you'll come downstairs and hang out for a little bit. You can't be so focused on work all the time and not have fun too, okay? I know you work hard because you want to save your mother, but I worry about you." She cupped his jaw and gazed into his eyes.

"I'll make time to have fun tonight. I'll come look for you in a bit."

She outright grinned then. "Good."

He watched her walk away, and relief lightened his shoulders.

Alone again, he ambled over to the window and surveyed the activity belowHis eyes returned to Monica, her bright smile in the camera, arm around her assistant as she livestreamed.

With a forceful exhale, he turned abruptly from the

window and sat at the computer to review the night's sales so far.

After tonight, he knew what he had to do. Even if he and Monica didn't get together, he couldn't continue his relationship with Belinda. It wasn't fair to her. He had to think of a way to end it so she didn't get hurt and everything didn't blow up in his face.

Chapter Seventeen

"We had a good night. The big man will be pleased," the bartender said.

Andre sat on a bar stool in his shirt and slacks, having removed his jacket after the venue emptied.

He nodded, confident Nigel would be ecstatic at the turnout and revenue from the night. "No doubt."

Belinda had left over an hour ago, and with all the guests gone, the bartender and Andre were the last employees on site.

The bartender gave him some dap. "Good job, man."

"Thanks for all your help."

He patted his pockets, fat with money from the tip jar. "All the thanks I need right here. See you tomorrow." He saluted Andre and sauntered toward the front door.

Andre sat in the silence, a sense of peace washing over him. Tonight had gone better than expected, and the experience had given him an idea of how to handle the opening of his own lounge in the future.

The sound of heels on the walnut floor drew his attention.

Monica walked toward him and immediately, his pulse jumped and spine straightened.

She stopped several feet away and placed a hand on her hip. "Well?"

"Well, what?" Andre asked, irrationally happy to see her at the end of the long night.

She stepped out of her heels and walked toward him, the shoes dangling from her fingers by the straps. As she placed one foot in front of the other, his eyes dipped to the sway of her hips. He couldn't help himself. This woman had him in a chokehold.

"How did the night go?" she asked.

"Better than expected."

"So you're pleased." Not a question. More of a statement.

"Definitely."

"I got a lot of interest during the live stream."

"A good number of folks used the code you gave out. I can run the exact figures tomorrow and let you know how many." Andre stood and went behind the bar. "Drink?"

"Sure." Monica set down her shoes and sat on a bar stool, resting against its wooden back. "Don't tell me you doubted me."

With a short laugh, Andre undid his cuffs and rolled up his shirt sleeves, exposing the tattoos on his forearms. "No way. I'd never doubt the great Monica Connor." He held up a tall, slender glass. "Dirty Shirley?"

"Yes, please."

Andre picked up a bottle of top shelf vodka. "With extra vodka."

"You remembered?" she asked, sounding pleased.

He lifted his gaze for a split second. "I remember every-thing about you."

He made the drink and set it in front of her. Then he poured himself a vodka on the rocks with a twist of lemon.

"To success." Monica held up her glass.

"I'll drink to that."

They clinked their glasses together and sipped at the same time.

"Mmm, good." Monica gazed across the bar, face animated, cheekbones pronounced in a soft smile, dark eyes focused on him in a way that could only mean trouble. He felt it in the air, weighing down on him.

Temptation.

"Where's your man?"

"I already told you, I don't have a man."

"So the guy you came here with, there's really nothing going on between you?"

"I didn't lie, Andre. He was someone to hang out with. A friend."

"Just a friend," Andre repeated.

"I take it Belinda went home already?"

Hearing his fiancée's name was a reminder he should be gone by now, slipping under the cool sheets of his bed to press against Belinda's soft body where she probably waited for him. Instead, he was planning to break her heart some time over the next day or two. Instead, he preferred to stand in the quiet, empty lounge, sipping a drink with the woman he couldn't get out of his mind.

"You look nice tonight," he said, avoiding talk about Belinda.

"I just threw this on," she said in a playful tone.

"That I doubt." His gaze lingered on her shoulders, and his loins became heavy with want. He swallowed more vodka.

Taking his time, he moved from behind the bar, and her eyes followed as she turned in a semi-circle on the stool.

"Why'd you come back, Monica?"

She gave a half-shrug. "I don't know."

"You know. Tell me why you didn't go home. Tell me why you're here. Why you're fucking with me."

Her eyes widened. "That's not what I'm doing."

"No? You know I'm still attracted to you."

"No, I don't."

"Did you forget what happened at the warehouse a few weeks ago? I haven't."

Face guarded, she didn't answer.

"You didn't forget, and you're still attracted to me. So why are you here right now?"

He stepped closer, and her body noticeably tensed.

"You gonna answer the question?"

"I was curious about how the night went," she said in a low, husky voice.

"What else?" He prodded softly. He shouldn't but couldn't stop.

He smelled her perfume and the unique fragrance of her skin. He used to like to bury his face in the crook of her neck and shower her with kisses until she giggled uncontrollably and begged him to stop. A long, long time ago. Why couldn't he forget?

"I guess I wanted to... hang out." She swallowed, chestnut-brown eyes gazing up at him.

"Why?"

"I don't know," she said in a low voice.

"Stop lying and tell me why."

Her shoulders squared, as if she suddenly made a decision. "Because I wanted to spend time with you, okay? I wanted to spend time with you, even if..." Her voice trailed off.

"Even if nothing could happen," Andre finished.

She took a swig of her drink and then cradled the glass in

her hand, resting it on her covered thigh. His gaze lingered on the split exposing the other. Finally, she nodded, keeping her eyes trained on the Dirty Shirley.

"You're playing a dangerous game."

"I know. I shouldn't have come back."

"No, you shouldn't have. We shouldn't spend time alone. Anything could happen."

She lifted her eyes, taking her sweet time to let her gaze travel up the front of his shirt, up his throat to his eyes. The slow crawl caused an electric charge to crackle between them and left him feeling as tightly coiled as a rattlesnake.

"You sound mighty confident."

"You disagree?"

"No," she said in a low voice.

"Might already be too late," Andre said in a strangled voice.

She inhaled a tremulous breath and dodged his gaze again. "I don't want you to do anything wrong. I don't want to do anything wrong."

"I don't believe you. I don't believe you came back to *not* do anything wrong."

"What I want..." She temporarily closed her eyes and shook her head, as if trying to dislodge the thoughts that filled it. When she looked at him again, her mouth and eyes were set with determination. "I don't want you to be with her. I want you to be with me. I want you for myself. *I'm* the reason we're not together. I want you to forgive me. I want you to—"

"Stop it," he growled. "My expulsion wasn't your fault. I took the blame because I wanted to."

"Then don't marry her! I don't want you to marry her." Her breasts rose and fell with labored breaths. "If you have doubts, you shouldn't marry her. You know I'm right."

She was right. He wanted her, and there was no way he could marry Belinda with the feelings he had for Monica. He was going to have to hurt Belinda and hated himself for it. In retrospect, had he ever really loved her? She had never consumed him the way Monica did. She had never made him want to put himself in harm's way and proudly bear the repercussions the way he would for Monica, without hesitation.

Andre placed his drink behind her, he lifted her drink from her hands, and placed it on the bar too. Then he did what he'd longed to do ever since they'd been interrupted at the old warehouse. He cupped her face with one hand, and she let out a soft sigh—a sound of relief—as if she'd been waiting centuries for him to make a move.

Edging closer, he pushed her knees apart.

"I'm not gonna marry her."

Her eyes closed, and she shakily whispered, "Andre."

"This what you want?"

Her lower lip trembled. "Yes."

He kissed her. Her petal soft lips drew him in. When her wet tongue touched the tip of his, his hands dropped to behind her knees, and he hauled her to the edge of the barstool and into the hardening flesh between his thighs. His tongue slid along hers to deepen the kiss. In the sweetness of her mouth he tasted the lemon and cherry from her drink.

She moaned and tipped back her head, and he pressed kisses to the swanlike curve of her throat. With her body angled over the back of the chair, he smoothed his hands up and down her thighs, savoring the softness of her skin.

She cupped him through his slacks, and it was his turn to moan. He shuddered, needing more.

His tongue swiped inside her mouth, his teeth nipping at the tender flesh of her lower lip. Each whimper and moan only propelled him to do more—deeper kisses, firmer caresses of her thighs and hips.

He reached higher and rubbed her pebbled nipples with

his thumbs and kissed down her neck. Her right leg locked around him, while her arms folded around his back and they kissed harder and hungrier.

Consumed by flames of lust, the sounds of their enthusiastic kissing filled the otherwise quiet restaurant. This kiss was rawer and more ravenous than the last.

He licked the side of her neck and sucked the pulse at her collar bone. She trembled and let out a torturous moan, and he knew then without a doubt, she was his for the taking. Right now, in this venue.

Lifting her, he switched places so he was sitting on the stool and her long legs straddled his lap.

"This fucking dress, I want to rip it to pieces," he rasped impatiently, shoving a hand high on her thigh. "You showed up in my life after all these years and my head is all screwed up," he said angrily.

"I'm sorry," she whispered, pressing her lips to his jawline and throat.

She sucked his neck, her fingers raking through his short hair. He gripped the flimsy G-string of her thong and curled his fingers around it, shaking with need as the urge to tear every article of clothing from her sexy body clamored through him.

Their mouths crashed together again, their kiss hard and long—her body undulating, her sex grinding on his hard dick. If they were naked, this would be the perfect angle to fuck her good and proper.

"Andre."

His name sounded distant and foreign. Confusion clouded his brain. He was kissing Monica, so she couldn't have called his name.

Two seconds later, sanity returned and he wrenched his mouth from hers and stared in dismay at Belinda. They had been so swept away by the heat of desire, neither heard her enter.

Monica froze and swore under her breath, her hands falling to his biceps. But she still straddled him, her dress pushed high on her thighs, his hands gripping her bare ass under the silky material.

Belinda stared at them with stricken, wide eyes. "What the hell are you doing?"

Chapter Eighteen

Monica hopped off his lap and right away started adjusting her clothes. Andre came to his feet slowly, eyes on Belinda. He expected her to be very upset and justifiably so. He didn't know what she would do.

"I knew it!" she spat, angry tears filling her eyes. "I knew there was something going on between the two of you."

Andre held up his hands to calm her down. "Monica and I are not—"

"Don't you lie to me! We're engaged. Doesn't that mean anything to you?"

"Of course it does."

"That didn't stop you from screwing her, did it?"

"We haven't had sex," Andre said, though he doubted the explanation would matter much to her. He'd wanted to end their relationship, but not this way.

"And you, you slut," she continued, upper lip curling in disgust. "Can't get your own man so you have to chase after someone else's?"

Monica's back straightened, and she opened her mouth to respond, but Andre touched her shoulder. "Don't. You should leave. Let me talk to her alone."

"She has no right to call me a slut. I am not a slut."

"Now is not the time, Monica," Andre said in a weary voice. How did he end up between two high-strung women with volatile personalities?

"Then what do you call a woman who sleeps with another woman's fiancé, huh? Do you like the word whore better? Or homewrecker?" Belinda taunted.

Monica took a step toward her. "If you don't—"

Belinda came toward her. "I don't want to hear shit from a bitch who—"

Andre stepped between them. "Ladies!" he hollered, holding up his hands to keep them apart.

They both fell silent. Belinda crossed her arms over her heaving chest, and Monica glared at her with tension in her shoulders.

"I need you to go," he said to Monica.

She shifted her glaring eyes to him. "She can't talk to me like that. I have a right to defend myself."

"Not now. Let me handle it."

"Andre—"

He grabbed her by the arm. "Go!"

If she didn't get out of there and let him calm the situation, they could very well go to the blows, and women fought dirty. No man with two brain cells wanted the dreadful task of separating two fighting women.

Monica's eyes widened, and her lower lip trembled. Then she yanked away her arm and skirted by Belinda, who edged sideways and muttered "Bitch" as she passed.

Monica's steps didn't hesitate. She kept moving and rushed

out of the lounge. Andre stared after her and noted her bare feet. She had left her shoes against the wall, running off like Cinderella, not escaping the ball—but escaping the ogre he'd become.

Belinda scowled at him with such fury, he wouldn't be surprised if she wished him dead.

"I can't believe you," she said.

Andre rubbed his hand over the crown of his head. Guilt and shame filled him in the midst of searching for the right words.

"I assumed you'd be here, working hard and working late. Because you'd want to check the numbers so you could let Daddy know how everything went. I knew as soon as I saw the white Porsche Cayenne parked outside she was here. I recognized it from her Instagram page. I came in quietly and caught you red-handed, you slimy son of bitch."

"Belinda, I'm sorry. I don't know what else to say, except that I'm sorry."

"Do you love her?"

"I..."

The answer stuck in his throat. Did he? He wasn't sure. A long time ago he had loved Monica deeply. To say he loved her seemed premature. He certainly couldn't get her out of his mind, and there was no question his attraction to her—their mutual attraction—had not diminished one iota.

"She and I have history," he said instead.

"I feel like I no longer know you," Belinda said.

There was no point in beating around the bush or hemming and hawing. He needed to be up front and tell her the truth—he wanted to end their engagement.

"Have I been putting pressure on you, because of the wedding?"

Like so many people who have been wronged, she looked at

herself to determine if she could be the cause of the problem, when in fact he was the only one to blame.

"You haven't put any pressure on me, Belinda. Matter of fact, you been pretty understanding, but you won't want to hear what I have to tell you."

She waited, body taut and braced for the impact of his words.

Andre paced the floor and then made eye contact. "I been trying to figure out the best way to tell you what I have to say, but the only way to tell you is to straight up say it. Belinda, you're a beautiful woman, and the past couple of years have been incredible, but our relationship has run its course."

She stared at him without any change in her expression.

"Did you hear what I said?" Andre asked.

She took a deep breath and audibly released it. "I heard you."

"I know this probably seems to have come out of nowhere, but—"

"No, it doesn't. I mean, I caught you with your tongue down another woman's throat and your hand up her dress. So it's a really odd thing to say that our relationship has run its course." Anger pulsed in her voice.

"I know, and I'm sorry."

"You asshole."

He deserved that. "I never meant to hurt you."

"And yet, you have. What am I supposed to tell people?"

"Tell them *you* dumped *me*, if you like."

She walked over to the bar and twirled his half-drunk vodka on the bar top. "No."

"No?" Andre didn't think he'd heard her correctly.

"How many times have you slept with her?"

"Despite what you saw, Monica and I haven't slept together."

She glared at him. "I. Don't. Believe. You. How many times?"

"Would you like me to lie?"

"If you haven't had sex with her, then this makes my decision easier. I forgive you."

"You... excuse me?"

"I forgive you." She shrugged. "You made a mistake, and now it's out in the open and I'm aware, and you realize how much it hurts me and that you almost lost me and everything I come with. I'm sure you won't do it again. Cut off all contact with her and everything can go back to normal."

Andre stared at her in shock.

She let out a shrill laugh. "This isn't a trick, Andre. I really do forgive you. You regret what happened, don't you? You agree it was a mistake?"

He stroked the tuft of hair on his chin. "It was a mistake, but not in the way you think."

She arched an eyebrow and waited for him to explain further.

"Monica and I haven't slept together, but I have feelings for her." Being blunt might be the only way to get through to Belinda.

Her right eyelid twitched. "Are you saying you're in love with her?"

"I'm saying I have feelings for her, and I can't go through with the wedding if I have feelings for another woman."

"Are you really going to break up with me, for her—a woman who came out of nowhere? We've been together for two years, Andre. You work with my father. You're not only giving me up, you're giving up all of this." She waved her hands wildly at the interior of the restaurant.

"The business doesn't matter to me," Andre said.

"Oh really? And what about your mother?"

129

The hard part, the worry his actions could cause the appeal to stall.

"I'll take my money and find another business to invest in," he said.

A bitter smile curled one corner of her lips. "Well, you have it all figured out. I guess I'll tell anyone who asks that I dumped you, as you suggested. No way I'm admitting someone like you dumped me."

His eyes narrowed. "Someone like me? What does that mean?"

She sniffed, lifting her nose higher in the air. "Let's be real, I was dating down when I started dating you. The reason my father asked you to open Midnight Lounge and considered making you a managing partner was because I asked him to. We both agreed it was a good idea so I could have a fiancé with a little bit of prestige."

Her ugly comments stung and went to the heart of the disdain he'd detected from other people when they learned about his past and his parents' records. Hearing Belinda, the woman he'd intended to marry, speak about him and his family in such a way infuriated him. She'd hidden her disdain well.

"You're a fucking snob."

"I'm a realist, so let's be real. You're a little rough around the edges, with the criminal background and your mommy being in jail and all. I saw someone I could mold and give a little class. My father liked you too, and the sex is great." She shrugged.

Had he known all along that she looked down her nose at him, he would have never become involved with her.

"I see the bitch gloves are off."

"Don't call me a bitch!" she snapped.

"If you don't like being called a bitch, then don't act like one," he retorted.

"You know what, you and that skinny heffa did me a favor. I'm glad I caught you two together, because now I know who you really are. You're a liar and a fraud, and you're lucky I ever had anything to do with your ghetto ass."

She seized the glass from the bar, and Andre flung his hand in front of his face right as she tossed contents at him. Vodka splashed onto his palm and dribbled down his face and onto his shirt. Droplets hit the wood floor.

With a self-satisfied smirk, Belinda lifted her head to a haughty angle and held up her left hand. "Don't even *think* about asking for this back. I consider it compensatory damages for all the pain and suffering you put me through. Good riddance."

She marched away, hips swinging and heels click-clacking on the wood floor.

Andre flexed his fingers in anger and breathed deeply to calm down. He took napkins from behind the bar and dried his face and hand. He cleaned up the spilled vodka from the floor and washed the two glasses he and Monica drank from.

After making one last pass through the restaurant, he flung his jacket over his shoulder and turned out the lights. The walk to the front door seemed longer. Perhaps because of the dark.

Or perhaps because he knew this was the last time he'd set foot in the Midnight Lounge.

Chapter Nineteen

Monica pulled her SUV into the driveway at the front of the house. Multiple cars were parked outside, and she recognized them as vehicles belonging to her siblings. Still shaken after the argument at the restaurant, she didn't want to see anyone right now, so she quietly entered the house and heard laughter coming from the direction of the den.

She crept up the stairs in her bare feet and almost reached her bedroom when she ran into Skye, Ethan's fiancée. She had tawny-gold skin, and her full figured body was currently covered in a pair of loose-fitting green pajamas, her hair lifted off her neck in a high ponytail. Last year, she and Ethan went through a difficult period and temporarily broke up, but their relationship was back to normal as they planned their wedding.

"Hey, we missed you at dinner. Bruno and Rodolfo cooked a delicious meal tonight. Oh my goodness, I'm still full." She patted her belly. "You coming downstairs? There's an intense game of charades taking place. Ignacio is cheating, as usual, mouthing clues to his teammates. You know how he is."

Ignacio was one of Monica's stepbrothers, an actor who often returned to Atlanta in-between filming, though he owned a place in LA.

Monica shook her head. "I have to pass," she said, mustering her best smile.

The effort didn't work because a frown descended on Skye's face.

"Hey, what's wrong?"

"I don't want to talk about it." Monica averted her eyes and bolted for her bedroom door.

Before she could close it, Skye pushed her way in, and Monica backed away.

"Talk to me."

Skye's gentle prodding was her undoing. Her face crumbled, and she covered her face with her hands as tears poured down her face.

"Oh, honey. What's going on?" Skye looped an arm around her shoulders and led her to sit on the edge of the bed.

"I don't know what I'm doing. I'm losing my mind." Monica sniffled and wiped tears from her cheeks.

"What happened?"

"This guy... he... I can't get him out of my head. We used to be a couple. Honestly, I consider him my first love, and ever since we ran into each other, I can't think straight. It's like someone is ripping my heart out."

"Sounds like you're in love," Skye said quietly.

Monica glared at her through watery eyes. "*No.* I am not in love."

"Then why are you crying?"

"We got caught kissing. Well, more than kissing, by his fiancée." She shook her head, disgusted with herself and her behavior.

"Oh," Skye said in a heavy tone.

Monica didn't look at her. She didn't want to see judgment on her face.

"Does he feel the same way you do?"

Contemplating the answer, Monica lifted her heels to the edge of the bed and wrapped her arms around her legs. "I don't know," she said honestly. "All I know is, I don't like feeling like this. It's not supposed to hurt." Her voice cracked.

"What isn't?"

"This. Whatever it is."

"You mean love?" Skye asked gently.

"I'm not in love with him, Skye. In lust, maybe. Love is... no." She shook her head vehemently and squeezed her legs tighter.

She couldn't be in love with Andre. After years apart, they barely knew each other now. Besides, Monica Connor did *not* believe in love and certainly wouldn't be foolhardy enough to fall for the man who'd broken her heart before.

"I don't want to feel like this anymore," she continued. "It hurts too much. He could be making up with her right now, thinking about the mistake he made with me. I can't believe how badly I messed up."

"Oh honey, I'm sorry."

Skye pulled her in for a side hug. Monica rested her head on her shoulder, wishing she had never run into Andre at the Chambers Enterprises office.

"You have to stop beating yourself up. You made a mistake, but you didn't make it on your own. He was involved too. Learn from it and move on. Tell you what, give me a few minutes to run downstairs and bow out of the games, and I'll be back so we can talk this through."

Although Monica appreciated her future sister-in-law's caring nature, she wanted to be alone. To think. To wallow in self-pity.

She lifted her head from Skye's shoulder. "No, don't do that. Go downstairs and enjoy yourself, but don't tell anyone about our conversation or that you saw me. I need time alone."

"You sure? I don't mind."

"I'm sure."

"Okay. You know I'm here if you need me."

"I know."

"I'll see you in the morning. Your mom, Audra, and I are making a big Southern breakfast. Grits casserole and biscuits and gravy are on the menu. We're also getting tomatoes from the garden to make fried green tomatoes."

Skye lost her parents when she was only a teenager, so spending time in the kitchen with Rose not only helped them bond, but she learned to prepare meals she'd never bothered to learn when her mother was alive.

"I'll be there ready to eat everything you guys make," Monica promised.

"Good." Skye squeezed her arm. "It'll get better, I promise."

Monica gave her a watery smile and then Skye exited the room.

Monica fell backward onto the mattress. Staring up at the ceiling, more tears trickled from the corner of her eyes.

Skye was right—it would get better. In the meantime, she resigned to suffering through the heartache of knowing her feelings for Andre were futile.

He wasn't a free man. He belonged to someone else.

* * *

Andre climbed out of the Escalade. A light shone through the bottom window of his apartment. He already knew who was in his apartment. He walked to the door and let himself inside.

He lucked out when he got this place, moving in when the

rents were much lower than the current market value. The one-bedroom, one and a half bath apartment was small in size but felt spacious because of the two-story ceilings.

The walls, painted terra cotta brown, evoked warmth and intimacy. To the left, he created a work out area with weights and a treadmill so he wouldn't have to go to the gym. To the right was a small kitchen with an L-shaped bar, where he sat on one of three stools to eat meals. Across from the kitchen, a living space contained two large couches so comfortable he'd fallen asleep on one or the other multiple times over the years, next to a huge window with a Colonial grid pattern taking up most of the wall and looking onto the street.

As suspected, Phin was inside peering into the refrigerator. His cousin paused to glance at him.

"What up, cuz?" he said, and resumed his inspection.

Everyone said they looked more like brothers than cousins. Same complexion and facial bone structure, but whereas Andre only sported a tuft of hair on his chin, his cousin had a full circle beard.

"Nothing much. What are you doing here this late?" Andre asked, though he already knew the answer to the question.

Phin often stopped by to eat his food, usually when Chelle was out of town.

"I need to ask you something."

Phin removed a pot of *rondon* from the refrigerator, a Nicaraguan soup dish made with seafood, vegetables, and coconut milk. One of the few dishes Andre's father had taught him to make, with the explanation that a man should learn to cook so he didn't 'have to depend on no woman to eat.'

Phin never learned that lesson. Chelle did all the cooking. Almost three years in, and his cousin couldn't function when his woman left town.

"You want this?" Phin asked.

"Nah, you can have it."

"Yeah, baby. I'm eating good tomorrow."

"What do you want to ask me? I'm tired, and I want to go to bed." Andre tapped his watch as Phin dumped the food into a plastic container he removed from the cabinet.

"My bad. Hang on."

He scraped the remnants from the pot and sealed the container. Then he put the pot in the sink. Andre didn't waste his breath scolding his cousin about washing it. Phin never did and if he did it now, the next time he wouldn't.

"I need your opinion on this." His cousin pulled a small black box from his pocket.

Whoa.

Shocked, Andre picked it up. Phin had never talked to him about marriage, though he shouldn't be surprised. His cousin was crazy about Chelle. Except, when he opened the box, inside were a pair of triple drop pearl earrings.

"Our third anniversary is coming up. I got a nice dinner planned at a restaurant we ain't never been to before. I hope the food is good. I did some research, and the third anniversary gift is leather. So I bought her this bad leather tote bag she could carry to work. I mean, it's nice, okay? I can't wait to see her face when she open the gift. I'ma put the earrings inside the bag for an extra surprise. What you think?" Phin waited, an expectant grin on his face.

"They're nice, but you need to remove them from this box." Andre snapped the box closed.

"What you mean? Why?"

"Because this looks like the box for an engagement ring, fool."

Phin covered his mouth. "Oh shit."

"Yeah. Think about it. She finds this, on your anniversary, at an expensive restaurant, and she'll think you about to propose. Then when she sees these earrings, she'll be real disappointed."

"You right, you right. Man, I'm glad I asked you. Good looking out."

"No problem. I'm going to bed. Lock up before you leave." Andre trudged toward the staircase.

"A'ight, man. Thanks again. Hey, how'd it go tonight?"

Andre paused. "Great. Big crowd and sales were ten percent higher than expected."

"Cool. Where Belinda at?"

Andre climbed the stairs. "At home."

"Later, man."

"Good night." Without turning around, Andre waved over his shoulder.

He walked across the narrow balcony to the frosted sliding door leading to his bedroom and let himself in. Once inside, he lay on the bed and stared up at the ceiling.

He didn't want to explain to his cousin about the fiasco at the restaurant. He'd save the Belinda-and-I-broke-up conversation for another day.

Chapter Twenty

What's this?

Shifting the plastic sack of groceries to his left hand, Andre peered down at the large UPS box at his front door. He saw the address for Chambers Enterprises and knew exactly what was in the box.

Inside, he placed the package on the kitchen bar and sliced it open, revealing the items from his office at the company headquarters. He couldn't be mad at the company. He'd done something similar, sending Belinda's clothes and other items to her house via messenger because he didn't want to see her face and deal with the drama.

With a cursory glance, he made sure all his belongings were in there, but instead of unpacking them, he moved the box to a corner and put away the groceries before going upstairs to his bedroom. He'd had a long day and needed a shower.

Andre stripped out of his clothes and stepped under the spray of warm water.

The day after he and Monica got caught, Nigel called. The conversation went pretty much as he expected. Nigel told him not to bother coming in to the office. The older man expressed his bitter disappointment, raging about how betrayed he felt. All to be expected. What Andre hadn't expected was for Nigel to accuse him of using the partnership to get close to Belinda and take advantage of her. Never mind Belinda had been the one to make the first move.

Nigel also implied that when he dissolved the partnership, there could be a delay in the return of Andre's money because of what happened between him and Belinda. The threat did not sit well with Andre. Up until that point, he had listened to the older man go off, taking the verbal beating because he'd done wrong. He did not, however, take kindly to the threat of withholding his money.

"If you know what's good for you, you'll give me money right away," Andre said, keeping his voice level.

"You should have thought about the consequences before you hurt my angel. Who knows how long this could take. Weeks? Months? Prepare to wait." Then he hung up.

Andre knew Nigel didn't have a legal leg to stand on, but he could delay solely to punish Andre. Which meant Andre would waste time and money fighting a man who had way more money than he did.

Stepping out of the shower, Andre rubbed his skin dry with a towel and then smoothed lotion onto his body. When he finished, he walked naked into the dark bedroom, still contemplating his options on how to deal with Nigel.

His phone vibrated and chimed on the table beside the bed, and Andre picked it up when he recognized the number. "Hello?"

"Hello, son, how are you?"

"I'm doing okay."

Smiling, he sank onto the bed. His mother, Priscilla Campos, secured a cell phone several years ago so they could talk regularly. She was calling earlier than usual. Normally she called well after lights out at the prison.

Each time he heard from her his spirits lifted. It meant she was alive and doing okay in that hellhole. While it was true his mother was aware of his father's illegal activities while he was alive, his father had been the career criminal, not her. He worried about her wellbeing in that place—mental and physical.

He could have so easily gone down the same path as his father, and was on his way there after his mother was arrested. At fourteen his best friend and only living parent had been reduced to a voice on the phone, and he never forgave himself for not saving his mother before she had to take matters into her own hands.

During the course of the trial, he'd bounced from family member to family member until his uncle, Phin's father, came from Atlanta to get him. At seventeen, he started a new life in a new place. He screwed up at first, running with the wrong crowd and getting himself in trouble there too.

Only after a particularly gut-wrenching phone call with his mother did he finally slow down. He listened to her pleas, as she sobbed on the phone.

Despite his delinquent activities, he was a good student and managed to earn a scholarship for late starters to UGA. The scholarship took care of tuition and work study took care of his housing. With a little help from his uncle and proud family members back in New York, the rest of his expenses were covered. When Andre had gotten kicked out, his family had been devastated, but nothing hurt more than hearing the disappointment in his mother's voice.

He missed her every day, but whenever she called, she couldn't talk long on the phone. He missed their long conversations, her unsolicited advice, and the way she teased him.

They talked for a few minutes, with his mother giving an update on the attorneys' progress. They'd recently filed papers they swore were key to getting the new trial, but she didn't understand all the details and legal jargon. She only knew they were waiting for a response from the court.

"What's wrong?" his mother suddenly asked.

"What makes you think something's wrong?"

"You don't sound like yourself."

Should he tell her? He didn't want to disappoint her anymore, but he also didn't like lying to his mother. "Belinda and I broke up."

"No, baby, what happened?"

They had the kind of relationship where he didn't need to hide the ugly truth. "She caught me with someone else."

A heavy sigh. "Andre, that's sloppy. You messed up your relationship for a side piece?"

"She's not a side piece." Andre released a deep breath, prepping for the fallout. "Matter of fact, she's someone from my past. I've told you about her before."

"Who is she?"

"Monica Connor."

During the silence, Andre rested his elbows on his knees and awaited his mother's tirade.

"Her again? She destroyed your life before."

"She didn't destroy my life before, Ma."

"Yes, she did. Listen, there are certain women who want men like you for the excitement of being with what they call bad boys. Then they move on. I wasn't sure about Belinda but figured you know best. Now your relationship is over, find a nice girl, like your cousin Phin did." Pause. "Andre, are you listening to me?"

"I hear you."

"So you're going to leave Monica alone?"

Andre didn't answer.

"You're not going to take my advice, are you?"

Silence.

Priscilla sighed heavily, and Andre imagined her shaking her head, the way she used to when he was a kid and did something wrong.

"You've always been so headstrong, like your father. You'll have to learn the hard way, I suppose."

"Don't worry about me. I know what I'm doing, Ma."

"I hope so. You're a man, old enough to make your own decisions—right or *wrong*. I have to go. I have to call your uncle, but I wanted to check on you since we hadn't talked in a while."

"Thanks for calling. The timing was perfect."

His mother let out a dry laugh. "I would believe that if you listened to me. I don't think this woman is good for you, baby. She let you take the blame for something she did." Another sigh. "I love you, all right?"

"I love you too."

When Andre hung up, he reflected on his mother's words and then mentally tossed them aside. The conversation had the opposite effect of what she wanted. He chose to take the fall for Monica. She didn't *let* him do anything, and he didn't care about imaginary repercussions of getting involved with her again.

Taking the fall for the drugs and kissing Monica—which resulted in losing Belinda and his investment income might— appeared to be errors in judgment. They weren't. In each case, he'd absolutely made the right decision.

That's why he dialed her number.

"Hello?" She answered quietly.

The sound of her voice messed with his head. He immediately became semi-erect.

"Hi, Monica."

"What do you want, Andre?"

You, he thought.

"You left your shoes at the lounge the other night. Thought you would have called by now to make arrangements to get them."

She was slow to respond. He waited.

"I thought about calling." She sounded hesitant. Not like the confident Monica he knew.

"Why didn't you?"

Another pause. "I don't know."

"Are you alone?"

He asked because he had been to her Instagram feed and saw a video of her, Daisy, and Donald Duck partying at a club in New York.

"Yes."

"I want to see you."

"No. Not while you're with her."

"Belinda and I are done."

"You broke up?" He heard the unmistakable breathless quality of her voice.

"Yes."

"When?"

"The same night. Friday night."

"Why didn't you call me before?"

"I needed to think, to sort through everything before I called you. Then I went to your Instagram feed and saw you partying with your *friend,* Donald."

"He *is* a friend, whether you believe me or not."

"I believe you. I don't like it, but I believe you." Silence. "Come get your shoes."

"Now?"

"Yes."

"What do you really want, Andre?"

"For us to finish what we started at Midnight."

"So this is a booty call?"

"It's minutes after eight. Too early for a booty call."

"I can't come. I'm at home, I'm comfortable and in for the night."

"I'm not asking, Monica. Come see me."

The silence at the other end of the line hinted she fought the urge to give in, but would eventually. He would, if she called and asked him to come see her. He'd drop everything.

"Text me the address."

The line went dead.

Elation thrummed through his veins. Andre immediately texted his address and then hauled on a pair of boxer briefs. Then he lit candles around the room and turned on a playlist of R&B music.

When Monica arrived, he greeted her at the door in nothing but his boxers, his anxious penis at half-mast. She wore a gray rib-knit cami dress. The stretchy material molded to her curves and brought attention to her small breasts and erect nipples.

"Damn."

That's all Andre could get out before he cornered her against the door.

"Where are my shoes?" she whispered against his lips, which hovered a couple inches from hers.

"In my bedroom." His gaze zeroed in on her plump lower lip, which he couldn't wait to suck.

"When do I get them?"

"Tomorrow, after breakfast."

His lips fastened on hers, and his hand went to her left breast. He sucked her bottom lip and nipped the soft flesh with his teeth. As he kissed her, he squeezed the soft flesh and thumbed the nipple. She moaned, a slight tremble running through her body.

Andre dragged the flimsy strap down her arm to reveal a perky nipple, which his mouth immediately closed over.

She arched against him, arms snaking around his neck as he sucked more of her flesh into his mouth, using his tongue to tease and taunt by circling the rigid peak in a relentless loop.

"Andre." His name tumbled out as a whimpering plea.

His tongue swiped his lower lip as he hauled the hem of her dress higher, fingers searching but finding nothing but soft skin. She'd come over there with no underwear on.

"You're a bad girl," he said huskily. He kissed her harder and lifted her from the floor.

Monica wrapped her legs and arms around him, sucking on his lips and stroking his face with eager fingers.

Slowly, he climbed the staircase with her in his arms.

Chapter Twenty-One

Monica washed her hands and exited the bathroom. Andre lay supine on the bed, eyes closed. The music had been turned off and the room was completely quiet.

Slipping under the covers, she asked, "Are you asleep?"

"No." His eyes opened.

Monica tugged the linens to her chest. "I can't believe I'm lying here with you."

Not that she'd had a choice. She didn't know the words self-control or boundaries where Andre was concerned. His words acted like a chain around her neck, dragging her to him against her will. He called, she answered. He requested, she gave. With him, all she knew to do was submit.

Andre turned onto his side, eyes going soft. "Lucky you."

"I see your ego is still intact."

She outlined his lips with the tip of her finger, and he flicked out his tongue and licked it.

"Stop," Monica said, giggling.

He rolled over and rested a hand on her hip, caressing from the hipbone to her butt and back again. "I'm glad you came."

"I came to get my shoes."

"And got sidetracked by my huge dick?"

"I swear your ego is out of control."

"I'm repeating what I've heard. People have always referred to it as *huge*. All caps."

"By 'people,' you mean you?"

They both laughed. She'd missed this comfortable feeling of being with someone who not only spiked heat in her blood, but who had the same sense of humor.

When the laughter died down, Monica traced the tattoo on his left pec. A collection of black stars wound in a swooping wave from the top of the muscle to the bottom. "This is new. You didn't have this back in college."

"No, I didn't. I got it because of my Grandpa Cy. It's a reminder of something he used to say. He was always dropping knowledge on us, and one of the things he used to do is encourage us to pursue our dreams. He said always shoot for the moon. Even if you miss, you'll be among the stars."

"I've heard that saying before. It's motivating."

"Definitely."

"Since you have that tattooed on your chest, can you explain why you didn't finish getting your degree?"

He groaned, clearly not wanting to talk about it. He'd been working toward a degree in hospitality management.

"Come on. You're smart, Andre."

"College ain't for everybody."

"True, but you did go, and you only have one year left to get your degree."

Staring up at the ceiling, he blew out a harsh breath. "I'm not sure why I never finished. Time was always a factor. Once I started working, I couldn't figure out how to fit studying into my day. Eventually, I figured I didn't need school."

"You were the first in your family to go to college."

"I screwed that up."

"Because of me," Monica said quietly.

"No." He spoke the word firmly and decisively. "I never blamed you for what happened because it wasn't your fault. I don't regret telling UGA the drugs were mine."

"Then why did you break up with me afterward?"

"It's complicated." He rubbed his palm back and forth across the top of his head, as if exhausted by the conversation.

"Explain it to me. I have time."

"Not now, Monica. Another day, okay?"

She didn't like his answer but didn't want to push.

"When was the last time you talked to your mother?"

"Hitting all the hot topics tonight, huh?"

"You know I don't run from issues."

"No, you don't. I talked to her tonight, actually, before I called you."

"How did she sound?"

"Surprisingly upbeat."

"That's good. How will your breakup with Belinda affect the money you have available for her defense?"

"It won't affect it in the short term, but in the long run..." His voice trailed off. "I don't want to let her down. I gotta figure something out. We're so close."

Monica kissed his shoulder and rubbed his chest.

"She told me I'm like my father."

Monica rested her head on the pillow. "Are you?"

"A little bit. Not as much as I used to be when I was wild as hell, acting out, and didn't care about nothing. I wanted to be like him, but everything I admired in him could get me into trouble."

"Like what?"

He paused before answering. "Like having a hair-trigger temper and being ready to go to blows over the slightest sign of disrespect. He commanded respect with his fists."

"Did he ever...?"

"Nah. He never hit on me or my mom or nothing like that. I'm talking about other people, you know? Competition on the block, that kind of thing. I also got my sales ability from him. My father could sell sand in the desert."

She laughed. "I wish I'd had a chance to meet him."

"Me too."

"Did you tell your mother about Belinda?" Monica asked in a softer voice.

"Yeah, she knows we broke up."

"Did you tell her it was because of me? Like the incident at UGA?"

"*I* make my own decisions. I told you, I don't blame you for what went down at UGA." He pulled her into his arms. "I don't care what anybody thinks about us. Do you?"

She gazed into his dark brown eyes and her world shifted. Sex with other men left her satisfied, but never with the same feelings she experienced with Andre. She opened herself up to him in a way she didn't with them. With Andre, sex transcended the mere act, landing her in a place of emotional completion.

Her heart clenched with the realization she was right where she belonged. Andre was it for her. The end of the road. She would stay with him for as long as he wanted her.

"No, I don't care what anybody thinks," she replied.

"Then you need to call your other men and tell them you're off the market. You know I don't play that sharing shit. So no one else, right?"

Monica pressed closer to him. "No one else," she agreed.

* * *

Andre finished getting dressed in black jeans and a fitted black shirt.

"You're going out?" Monica's sleepy voice came from the bed.

"I'm going to the office."

"To Chambers Enterprises?" she asked, sounding surprised. "Did Nigel call?"

"No, but I'm going to see him. I won't be long." He slipped his gold rings onto his middle fingers. "I'll stop at Notte and pick up dinner."

"Sounds good." Monica yawned and stretched.

"Anything you want in particular?" he asked.

"Surprise me."

Andre strolled over to the bed, his heart full as he observed Monica in his bed. Having her here made every negative thing that had happened worth it. "Go back to sleep. I know I been wearing your ass out."

"You have, you animal." She grinned up at him.

Andre kissed the top of her head, and the soft coils of hair tickled his lips.

"Bye," she whispered, before closing her eyes.

Andre slipped out the door and stepped onto the balcony. He jogged down the stairs and went straight to his workout area and retrieved his baseball bat from the corner.

Late last night he figured out how to handle the situation with Nigel. He was done being nice and tired of pretending to be someone he wasn't—a person who would lay down and take whatever some asshole dished out. He wasn't proud of how his relationship with Belinda ended, but that didn't give Nigel the right to hold his money and make life difficult for him.

Nigel's obstinance meant the attorneys' work would have to

stall, and Andre couldn't let that happen. He had failed his mother once. He would not fail her again. He needed his goddamn money, and he'd channel his father to get it. His father would never tolerate this type of disrespect, and neither would he.

Nigel often worked late on Thursday nights because he liked to take off early on Fridays, so now was a good time to go over to the office. Most, if not all, of the staff would be gone, which meant he could talk to his former partner without other eyes and ears being present.

He climbed into the Escalade and blasted a rap song to get his blood pumping.

Andre parked in front of the building and tapped the glass on the locked door. The female receptionist, who confirmed via text that Nigel was working late tonight, opened the door. She had hung around to let him in.

"He upstairs?" he asked.

She nodded, casting a worried glance at the bat in his hand.

"Go," he said.

She hurried out the door, and Andre locked it.

The quiet all around him meant no one was downstairs, and he hoped the third floor was equally empty. He walked with purpose to the elevator but changed his mind and took the stairs. On the third floor, he paused when he exited the door. Quiet up here too.

He made a beeline for Nigel's office. He shoved open Nigel's door so hard, it slammed against the inner wall, and a startled Nigel gaped at him with the phone to his ear.

"Hang up," Andre said, standing with his legs shoulder width apart.

"I'm going to have to call you back," Nigel told the person on the other line. He carefully placed the phone in the cradle.

"What are you doing here, and why do you have a bat in your hand?"

Andre gripped the bat's handle with his right hand and bounced the barrel in his left. "I want my money."

"I told you, it's going to take time," Nigel said with surprising obstinance.

"I'm not satisfied with that answer." Andre swung the bat and shattered the lamp on Nigel's desk. Glass shards burst in the air and collided into the bookshelf before scattering across the carpeted floor.

Nigel cried out in alarm. "What the hell do you think you're doing!" he screamed.

"Communicating my displeasure with your answer. I want my mother fucking money. Not months from now. Not weeks from now. Tomorrow, deposited into my account. The full amount, with my share of the profits."

Nigel rolled his leather chair backward and hit the wall behind him. "You're asking for the impossible. I can't come up with that kind of money by tomorrow. Quite frankly—"

Andre swiped Nigel's computer and his pen and pencil holder off the desk with a single swing.

"You're insane! I'm calling the police."

One hard blow smashed the phone. Then Andre knocked it off the desk onto the floor.

He continued swinging the bat around the office. He broke apart a small side table and smashed framed photos from the wall. He broke the shelves on a bookcase and shattered Nigel's display of glass awards, sending them to the floor in a spray of fragments.

Nigel jumped to his feet. "Stop! Stop!" His voice quivered.

Andre barely contained his disgust. He wasn't remotely winded. He was just getting started.

"You have a different answer for me?" he asked, eyes narrowing.

Nigel was lucky he wasn't crazy like his father, or his face would be getting destroyed instead of the objects in the room.

"Y-yes," Nigel said, swallowing hard.

"When do I get my money?"

"T-tomorrow. I'll have it wired into your account."

"What a surprise. I guess it's not impossible after all. I'm sure you'll include my share of the profits?"

"Yes." Nigel nodded vigorously.

"I'll need a copy of the financials too." He no longer trusted Nigel and was entitled to those numbers. After he went over them, he would have Phin review the numbers a second time.

"Of course."

Andre lowered the bat, and Nigel clutched his chest in relief.

"Thank you. All I wanted was what's mine," Andre said.

"You'll have it all tomorrow," Nigel promised.

Andre stepped right up to the desk, and Nigel shrank against the wall, throwing his hands up, palms out, like someone under arrest. Reaching across the desk's surface, Andre pressed the end of the bat to the middle of the other man's chest.

"You're not gonna call the cops, are you?"

"Of course not." Nigel swallowed.

"Good. I look forward to getting my money. Don't let me down, Nigel. Or I'm coming back, and next time, I'm bringing friends."

He lowered the bat and walked out.

Chapter Twenty-Two

As the movie ended, Monica was oddly still and quiet in Andre's arms, her head resting on his chest as they laid in bed.

The past few days had been idyllic. Friday morning, Monica went home and came back with her assistant toting clothes for several days. Without asking—because why would Monica Connor ask permission?—she cleared space in one of his drawers for her belongings and hung two dresses in his closet. There were also four more pillows on his bed—way more than he needed, but who was he to argue?

Monica hadn't left since, and as a result, he'd barely gotten any work done toward researching a new investment strategy. He spent all his time with her. They ate together, made love, watched TV, and went out for drinks.

Last night he escorted her to the launch of a new perfume in New York. The whole event had been a fascinating display of excess, with media and photographers capturing photos of Monica and a model endorsing the new fragrance.

The company had paid Monica two hundred and fifty

thousand dollars to post one time about the perfume on her socials, and they flew her first class to promote in person. He and her assistant, Daisy, joined her on the trip.

He used to think being an influencer was easy work, but seeing behind the scenes changed his mind. A one minute video could mean hours of work because of set up, multiple takes, and editing. Then there was the issue of picking the right wardrobe, doing makeup, and meetings—all of which helped him develop a newfound respect for Monica's endeavor. Seeing her in her element at the fragrance launch notched his admiration higher. She smiled a lot and charmed the media with her jokes, all the while making sure the photogs captured her best angles. She was good at what she did. So good, she made her job look easy.

When Andre felt moisture on his right pec, he muted the television.

"Monica," he said.

"Hmm?"

"I know you not crying."

"I'm not," she lied through a wobbly voice.

"Let me see." Andre shifted in the bed and tried to tilt up her face, but she turned away.

"No!" She shoved at him, but he was stronger.

"Let me see." He rolled her onto her back and lay between her legs.

Roughly, she swiped away her tears.

"Why are you crying?" he asked, amusement in his voice.

"Don't laugh at me!"

"I'm sorry, Sunshine, but your emotional ass—"

"I'm not emotional. The movie was sad. Jerk! Get off me."

"Okay, you're right, it was sad. Most people wouldn't cry, though, so you are emotional."

156

He bent to kiss her lips, but she turned her face toward the patio door, and he kissed her cheek instead.

"Let me kiss you," he said, trapping her hands on either side of her head.

"No."

Andre tried again, and she craned her neck to escape his mouth.

"No. I mean it. You're mean to me."

He dropped tender kisses on her neck and clavicle. "I like that you're sensitive. It's sweet. You taste good too." He licked her neck and groaned.

She side-eyed him.

"I'm serious. Now give me some sugar."

"You only said that because you want a kiss."

"Not true. I mean it."

She hesitated, then she gave him a kiss.

"Thank you. Emotional ass."

Monica screamed in anger and he laughed, rolling off her. She picked up a pillow and beat him until he wrestled it away and dragged her down on top of him, locking down her arms.

"There you go, hitting again. Behave," he said.

"You get on my nerves," she said.

Andre kissed the top of her head, and she relaxed, settling against his shoulder. He rubbed a hand up and down her back. She wore a white cami and blue cheeky, and he let his hand slide lower to stroke the underside of her exposed bottom in the revealing underwear. He was so lucky she walked around like that, giving him an eyeful. So many women let insecurities keep them from displaying their bodies to their man, not knowing that simply being there was enough.

"I can't believe we spent the whole day in bed," Monica mumbled.

"It's Sunday and we needed the rest. Flying to and from New York in one day was a lot."

"My schedule can be crazy. Not always, though."

He turned off the TV and pressed his lips to her forehead. He found himself always kissing her. He couldn't remember ever being so affectionate with anyone else. "Good night."

"Good night," Monica whispered.

He was almost asleep when she stirred. "Andre?"

"Mmm?"

"What else do you like about me?" she asked.

"What?"

"Before, you said you like that I'm sensitive. What else do you like?"

"Everything, baby. You're sense of humor, for one. Then of course, there's your entrepreneurial spirit. You work hard." He lowered his voice and added, "And I love your sexy body."

"Do you really think I'm sexy?" In the ambient light, she gazed at him.

"Of course. You can't tell by how I'm always jumping your bones? Why would you ask me that?"

"Because."

"Because what?"

"My breasts are so small. I'm the chairman of the itty bitty titty committee."

He let out a soft laugh. "They're fine."

"No, they're not. I've always been self-conscious."

"I had no idea. I thought you were confident."

"I am, but everyone has something they don't like about themselves."

"Not me. I like everything about me."

Monica rolled her eyes.

"Okay, fine. I wish I wasn't so handsome."

"You know what..."

He laughed and squeezed her closer, nuzzling her neck and planting a kiss on the side of her throat. Damn, he really couldn't help himself. He had to kiss her all the time. "On a serious note, I think my calves are too small."

"What?" Monica propped up on one elbow to stare down at him.

"You heard me."

"That's crazy. I love your legs. You have sexy calves." She ran her toes up the back of his leg.

"Thank you. Now, back to you and this issue with your breasts. When did you develop this insecurity?"

She returned her head to his shoulder. "I don't know. Probably when I realized I would never have breasts like my mother and Audra. They're both short and have nice-sized boobs. Especially Audra. She has breasts-es-es."

He laughed.

"You noticed, didn't you?"

He'd seen photos of her sister and she did have a nice rack, but he knew to tread carefully. "Well..."

Monica shot him a warning look.

"Nah. I didn't notice."

They both laughed.

"You're a liar. Do better."

"The size of your breasts really bothers you?" Andre asked. Women never ceased to amaze him. If only they knew most men didn't give a shit about the issues they worried about.

"Yes. One time I made an appointment to get breast implants."

Andre shifted so they faced each other but kept one arm thrown across her waist. He couldn't believe what he was hearing. "Seriously?"

"I chickened out at the last minute and canceled my appointment. What would you think if I did get larger breasts?"

"Nothing, really. If it makes you happy, go for it, but don't go overboard and make them disproportionate to your body."

"So you would like it if I got bigger breasts?" she asked, watching him closely.

This was definitely a minefield, so he picked his words carefully. "I wouldn't be mad, but it's not necessary."

"If I got bigger breasts, would you think it was weird?"

"Personally, I don't care. I like all of you, the way you are."

A big grin spread on her face. "You wouldn't change a thing?"

"Not one thing. Matter of fact..."

He pulled her shirt over her head and started licking her breasts and kissing her nipples, moaning to point out how much pleasure her body gave him.

"Perfect," he whispered. "I can't stand SBB's."

"What are SBBs?" Monica asked, breathless.

"Saggy boob bitches."

She giggled and wrapped her arms around his neck.

He hugged her. "You can go braless in the summer, which means one less item of clothing I have to remove. I like everything I have right here, okay?"

"Okay. I guess there's nothing wrong with both of us having to settle."

"Both of us?" He frowned. "What are you talking about?"

"Well, you know, since I have to put up with your micro dick, why shouldn't you be satisfied with my small breasts."

"Micro—" Andre raised onto his knees and pulled out his semi-erect penis. Holding it in one hand, he asked, "This is what you calling a micro dick?"

Monica shrugged. "I've seen bigger," she said with wide-eyed innocence.

"Oh really? Okay, well go back to your Shaka Zulu-dicked

Negroes then." He tucked his penis back into his underwear and rolled onto his side, away from her.

"Baby, I'm kidding." Monica flung herself on top of him, throwing one leg across his hip. She kissed his ear and neck.

"Get off me."

"No."

"Get off me. I mean it now."

"No. No. No." With each No, she dropped a kiss on the side of his face.

Andre rolled over suddenly and she squealed. Settling between her legs, he brought his face down to hers. Settled between her warm thighs, he grew harder and longer.

"What's that?" she whispered.

"That micro dick you were talking about."

"Can I have some micro dick? I mean your *huge* dick, all caps."

He dropped his voice lower. "I shouldn't give you any. You don't deserve my extra-large, humungous penis."

She snorted in laughter, and he chuckled along with her.

"Did I say something funny?" he asked.

"Nope."

Andre kissed her gently, tracing a path from the middle of her forehead to the tip of her nose.

"You know what I want?" he asked.

"What?"

"I want to make love to the chairman of the itty bitty titty committee."

"Well, it so happens, she's free."

He lowered his mouth and kissed her lips. The tender kisses became more intense the longer their mouths stayed together. Monica locked her legs around his hips, grinding her pelvis against his.

Andre sucked her arched throat, and she moaned her satisfaction, arching her body higher. Peeling off her panties, he tossed them over the side of the bed before scooting below the sheets. He kissed around her navel and the crease of her hips before pressing his face between her thighs. He would stay down here all night if she let him.

His moist mouth worked the lips of her sex and plucked at the hard pearl nestled between them. The sound of her ragged breathing filled the room as he continued to taste and tease.

With his hands and mouth and tongue—and ultimately his penis—he showed her exactly how much he enjoyed every inch of her body.

Chapter Twenty-Three

Andre heard movement downstairs and knew only one person could possibly have entered his apartment without an invitation. A quick glance at the time, and he saw it was almost noon.

He quietly groaned. He needed to cut back on these late nights out with Monica. The party they went to last night had been a Hollywood party at some rich guy's house. Her actor stepbrother had acquired invitations for her. They didn't leave until almost four, and only because Andre made her leave. The party was still going strong when they left the mansion.

He eased away and Monica made a soft sound of discontent and rolled onto her other side, but she slept hard. Crashing cymbals couldn't wake her when she was deep in sleep.

He reluctantly left the warmth of the bed and the softness of her body and pulled on a pair of shorts and a gray T-shirt. He slipped into the bathroom to wash up, and when he came out, he paused for a moment and looked down at her, curled on her side.

She appeared peaceful in sleep, lush lips slightly parted,

her slender body barely visible beneath the rumpled covers. She was so different from her public persona, and he liked knowing he saw a side of her not everyone had the privilege of seeing. Monica wasn't only a party girl flying on chartered planes and lounging on yachts docked in exotic locations. She was kind, considerate, and sensitive and cared about other people's feelings. There was a lot more to her than she let on.

Andre jogged barefoot down the stairs, and sure enough his cousin Phin was in the kitchen. He held a large red bowl in his hand and spooned cereal into his mouth.

"Hey, good morning," he greeted Andre, as if he lived there.

"Chelle out of town again?" Andre sat on a stool across from him.

"Yeah, you know how it is."

"Yeah, I know how it is. You're completely helpless when your woman is out of town. She has you way too spoiled. You know you can order food, right?"

"Why would I when you always have a packed fridge? Except things are looking kinda sparse in there today. You need to go to the store. You ain't got no deli meat, no bread, no nothing for me to fix a sandwich with, man. Not no leftovers from eating out. I'm stuck eating cold cereal for lunch. You out of Cheerios, by the way."

Andre glared at him.

"And almond milk," Phin added.

"You don't like almond milk."

"I didn't have a choice. That's all you ever buy now. Ever since you took up with your bougie fiancée, regular milk ain't good enough for you no more."

"Or you can buy your own goddamn food."

"But your food is free. What's on the agenda for the day?" He lifted an overflowing spoon into his mouth and wiped away the milk dribbling down his chin.

"I'm busy today."

"Doing what? You and Belinda got plans?"

"Nah. Actually, me and her broke up."

Phin's eyebrows flew higher. "Say what now?"

"Wasn't working out."

"Wasn't working out? Bruh, you had the perfect set up. A rich female, her daddy love you, and you were an investor in his business, destined to become a full partner. Please tell me you didn't throw all of that away."

"It's complicated." Andre rubbed a palm across his unshaved cheek.

"Explain it to me like I'm five. Break it down for me."

Andre glanced over his shoulder toward the bedroom and lowered his voice. "There's someone else."

Phin's eyes widened and his eyes flicked toward the bedroom before returning to lock with Andre's.

"You cheated on her?"

"I didn't cheat on her." Well, that was a gray area which he had no intention of getting into with his cousin.

"But you got another bitch in here already though."

"Man, what'd I tell you about calling women bitches?"

"I'm sorry, damn. You got another woman in here already?"

"Yes."

"Do I know her, or is she brand new? No, don't answer. I already know. She's brand new. Managing those venues for Chambers had to be tempting with all them fine, educated honeys coming up in there all the time. That's why Chelle don't let me go nowhere without her. The temptation is too great."

"She's not new. You don't know her, but you know of her."

"What dat mean?"

"It's Monica Connor."

Phin dropped the bowl on the counter with a thud. "Aw, hell no!"

"Keep your voice down."

His cousin silently fumed while shaking his head. "Please tell me you're joking."

"I'm not joking."

"Monica Connor. Really, dawg? That woman is your only weakness. Ever since back in the day, she fucked up your whole life."

"Calm down. We reconnected and doing casual right now."

"Casual my ass. You know good and damn well you can't do casual with her." Phin shoveled more cereal into his mouth.

"I'm a grown ass man. Not some sixteen-year-old getting his first nut."

"You wasn't sixteen years old in college, either, but she got you to give up your whole life. Damn, man." Phin shook his head again as he ate more cereal.

"You know you could be happy for me, right?"

"You gave up Belinda, a sure thing. Oh, and I bet that means you're not an investor in Chambers Enterprises anymore, right?"

"Not at the moment," Andre admitted reluctantly.

Phin laughed. "What is it with this chick? She's the only woman I've ever known you to lose your mind like this over."

"I haven't lost my mind," Andre grated, aggravated.

Phin leaned across the counter. "Negro, you don't have a woman or a job or any kind of investment other than a few stocks you playing with."

"I'll be fine. By the way, I need you to stop using your key to come in here like you been doing."

"Why can't I come over no more? You want me to starve?"

"I didn't say you couldn't come over any more, but you can't be coming in here like you own the place. You need to call first. Monica's here a lot, more than Belinda."

"Great, now she fucking up my shit."

"Or I could take the key."

"No need for all that. We good." Phin muttered something under his breath. "So what's the plan. I know you got a plan working."

"Actually, I do have an idea I want to run past you. First, I need you to review the Chambers Enterprises financials for me to make sure Nigel's not screwing me over. He gave me a new login so I can access the system at the office, and I've already reviewed them, but I want another set of eyes to makes sure I didn't miss anything."

"Not a problem."

"Cool. Now, I've been working on a business plan for the lounge I want to open, but I need help—a polished proposal to take to the bank, to apply for a loan."

"I can help you with that. Matter fact, I have templates from my old job we can use to drop the data into and make the plan all pretty. We'll knock the banker's socks off. They'll be throwing money at you."

Part of Phin's duties at his old job was to review client business plans. He was a whiz with numbers and organizing the research in a way that acted as a guide for the clients and presented a neat package for the banks.

"I don't know about all that. I need a lot because of the renovations for the place I want to buy, but if everything works out, I'm going to need a business partner—someone to help me with the books. You interested?"

Phin's eyes widened. "You serious?"

"There's nobody else I'd rather do this with. If it's successful, we'll be successful together."

167

"Man, you gone make me cry like a bitch—I mean, woman."

Andre laughed. "Is that a yes?"

"You better believe it."

They gave each other some dap to seal the deal.

Phin cleared his throat. "Hey man, I never told you this, but the reason I decided to go to college was because of you."

Andre's eyebrows shot skyward. "I didn't know that."

"It's true. When you got your scholarship money, I thought —hey, I could go to college too, you know? Never thought about going until I saw you do it. I figured I'd be working in retail or work construction like my pops. He makes decent money, but it's hard work. I ended up sitting in an air-conditioned office, wearing ties to work and making bank. Everybody thinks folks get into college because they're smart. Don't nobody think that maybe a lot of those folks have opportunities we don't. We're just as smart, you know? We just need a shot. It took seeing you take your shot to make me want to get my grades up."

"Yeah, but I messed up."

"Wasn't your fault though. Anyway, now you got a second chance. I know you're getting NV Lounge off the ground."

"I'm not going to blow it," Andre said with confidence.

"What was it Grandpa Cy used to say? It's never too late to be what you coulda been. It ain't too late, Dre. If anybody can do it, I know you can."

"Thanks, man."

There was an awkward moment of silence before Phin said, "Enough sappy talk."

He drained the sugary milk from the bottom of the bowl into his mouth. Then he dropped the dishes in the sink.

They chatted for a while, catching each other up on family news. Phin also let Andre know that Chelle loved the earrings and bag he gave her for their anniversary, and according to him, she loved the bag so much she took it every-where. He showed Andre a nice leather wallet she'd purchased for him, and she'd gifted him with a day at a male spa. After about thirty minutes of conversation, Phin checked the time.

"I better go. My appointment at the spa is in an hour, but I need to stop at home first. You know, when Chelle first gave me the gift card, I didn't like the idea of going to a spa and being pampered or whatever, but then I read the reviews. I think I'm in for a good time. I'm really looking forward to the hot stone massage, and I'ma get scrubbed and exfoliated so my skin is soft and supple for when my baby comes back." Moving to his own private music, Phin did a two-step dance to come out from behind the bar.

Before Andre could respond, his cousin lifted his gaze toward the staircase. Over his shoulder, he saw Monica descending the stairs. She wore large hoop earrings and a neck-lace with a heart-shaped pendant over a white tank top that fit tight and showed off her slender torso, while distressed denim shorts displayed her long legs to full advantage. Strappy sandals with a block heel, a Gucci tote in the crook of her right arm, and oversized Gucci sunglasses over her eyes completed the outfit.

She looked fabulous.

"Good afternoon." She smiled at both men, sidling up to Andre, who had come to his feet.

He slipped an arm around her waist and resisted the urge to kiss all over her in front of his cousin. "Monica, this is my cousin, Phin. Phin, this Monica."

"Hi," she said, extending a hand.

"The infamous Monica," Phin said, shaking it.

"Infamous?" She glanced at Andre.

"Please don't start no shit," Andre warned his cousin.

"My bad. I've heard so much about you, Monica. Nice to finally meet you."

"Nice to meet you too." She turned to Andre, lowering her voice. "I've gotta run. You sure you don't want to come with me?"

She was on her way home, and last night she had invited him to come with her, but the offer didn't appeal to him.

"I need to get some work done," he said.

She pursed her lips in disappointment. "Okay. I'll see you later." She lifted her arm around his neck and they kissed, Andre sliding his hand lower to steal a squeeze of her bottom.

"Bye," he said, gazing into her eyes.

"Bye." She glanced at Phin. "Bye."

His cousin nodded.

Monica strutted across the floor and with one final wave, exited to the outside. Andre had kept his eyes on her the entire time, and when he returned his attention to his cousin, Phin was shaking his head.

"You whooped."

Chapter Twenty-Four

The house was quiet when Monica entered. She came home to spend time with her mother, but it seemed as if she wasn't there. She passed through the three arches leading to the rest of the house and ran into Giselle.

She wore a white shirt and black, neatly pressed pants, her hair braided in fresh cornrows secured at the nape.

"Hi, Giselle. Do you know where my mother is?"

"Miss Rose is in the garden," Giselle replied.

"How long has she been out there in this heat?"

"Over an hour. She's weeding today."

Monica sighed. Her mother loved her garden, and she understood the desire to stay active but didn't like her mother working out there for long periods. The saying *once a man and twice a child* made perfect sense in relation to her mother. At some point, children had to look out for their parents' wellbeing and take care of them. Rose acted as if she was in her twenties and needed to be careful she didn't dehydrate. Each member of the family had scolded her at one point or another, but she never listened.

"Where is everybody else? Bruno and Skye?"

"I'm not sure where your brother is. I haven't seen him since yesterday, but he did mention he needed to check on the renovations at his house. He might be there. Skye won't be here until later this afternoon. She and your mother are going to visit possible venues for the wedding."

"Thank you." Monica made a beeline toward the stairs.

"Oh, your Aunt Florence is here somewhere."

Monica's lips flattened in displeasure, and the corners of Giselle's mouth tipped upward, doing a poor job of hiding her amusement. Monica and her Aunt Florence tended to bump heads.

"Thanks for the warning," she said.

"You're welcome, ma'am."

Monica continued to her room and rested her Gucci bag on the table by the window. She changed shoes and then ran downstairs to the kitchen, where she took a chilled bottle of water from the refrigerator and went out to the terrace. She saw her mother in the distance.

Using a hand to provide shade, Monica squinted against the sun's rays and walked across the property to her mother's side. Rose wore a wide-brimmed hat, a pink T-shirt, and baggy, washed out jeans rolled up at the ankles. Upon closer inspection, Monica guessed the denim pants were an old pair of her stepfather's that her mother had commandeered for outside work.

"Hi, Mommy."

Rose straightened from her position bent over the ground, and smiled at Monica. She wiped sweat from her brow with her forearm. "Hi, honey."

"How long have you been out here?" Monica extended the bottle of water.

"Don't start with me. I've only been out here... maybe an

hour or so. I wanted to finish what I started yesterday." She removed her garden glove from one hand and dropped it into the basket beside her with the weeder and garden knife. She took the water and tipped her head back, drinking quite a bit before letting out a satisfied *ahhh*.

"How many times do I have to tell you when you come out here, make sure you have water? If you don't, at least work in frequent breaks."

"Give me some credit. I listen to my body, and I know when I've done too much."

"I want you to be careful. Record-breaking heat is not the norm. This is not the sun you grew up working under."

Rose laughed. "Yes, ma'am."

"I'm not kidding. If you don't listen to me, I'm telling Papa Ben." He had threatened to hire a full-time gardener if Rose didn't act right.

"You would rat out your own mother?"

Monica stared at her in defiance.

"Oh for goodness' sake. Fine! I will be more careful."

"Thank you," Monica said with a triumphant smile.

Her mother looked her up and down and her expression softened. "I'm glad to see you. How long will you be home?"

"Not long. I came home so we could hang out tonight."

"I can't. I'm going with Skye to two or three venues for the wedding, and then we're going to dinner."

"Giselle told me."

"You should come with us."

"No, thank you on checking out the venues, but I'll meet you for dinner afterward."

"You're not going to get cooties if you come to the properties with us."

"It's not my thing. I'll be happy to meet you afterward," Monica repeated.

"All right. I should call Audra and see if she's free and would like to join us. Your Aunt Florence is here, we can all have dinner together." Rose's eyes brightened. Pulling family together was one of her favorite things.

"Sounds like a plan. I'll see you later. Don't stay out here too long."

"I won't, sweetie. Thank you for your concern."

Monica went back up to the house and happened to glance in at the great room and see the wedding magazines on the table. Her footsteps slowed to a stop. Seemed like the collection had increased since she last saw them.

Out of curiosity, she went into the room and picked up a copy of *Brides*. Flipping through the pages, she paused every now and then to admire the dress designs. The women's expressions ranged from subdued pleasure to flagrant happiness, and the ones posing with a groom had a starry-eyed expressions.

Good job looking as if you're in love with the model working beside you, she thought cynically.

She turned a page and froze, inhaling sharply at the next dress in a nontraditional color. The Queen Anne bodice would look great with her shoulders. Strapless and blush-colored, the floor length gown was a dreamy vision of tulle with oversized flower-inspired prints throughout the full skirt.

She'd never imagined herself in a wedding dress before, but a vivid image of her at the front of a church in *this* dress, came to mind. Andre stood at her side and gazed at her with adoration—the way he always did—which made her heart constrict.

Emotion flooded her system. Her throat tightened. What was wrong with her? She didn't care about this stuff. She didn't care about wedding dresses, marriage, or babies.

With a start, Monica had the feeling she was being watched. The hairs on the back of her neck stood on end, and she swung toward the door. Sure enough, Aunt Florence hovered in the doorway.

"Considering your aversion to marriage, I hope you don't spontaneously combust," her aunt remarked in a dry tone.

Of all the people to catch her looking at the magazine... Monica groaned inwardly and dropped it on the table. "Hi, Auntie."

Aunt Florence shuffled into the room, and one eyebrow lifted higher than the other. She was her mother's older sister— short and spunky and always wearing a hat. Today she wore a wide-brimmed sun hat, an ivory color that matched her ivory linen pants and went well with the loose-fitting yellow shirt.

"Having a change of heart?" her aunt asked.

"Why would I do that?"

"Your mother seems to think you have a new boyfriend. You've been at home less than usual."

"I do have a friend I'm spending time with," Monica admitted.

"It must be serious then."

"You know me. I'm never serious about anyone." She smirked.

"Why not?"

The unexpected question took her aback, but she had an answer.

"Auntie, there are so many men in the world. Why settle on one when none of them have all the qualities I'm looking for?"

"Is that right?" Her aunt sounded amused, which grated on Monica's nerves. "What qualities are you looking for?"

She did not want to have this conversation with her aunt but decided to humor her. "He has to be good-looking—to me at least. Physical attraction is important."

Aunt Florence nodded her head. "Go on."

"Trustworthy."

This characteristic might very well be the most important. In her world, trustworthy people were difficult to come by. She'd been burned enough times by so-called friends and shady business associates, which meant she guarded the good ones like a pit bull.

Andre had fallen short in the trust department. *Forever with you ain't enough.* He'd barely lasted a year before breaking her heart. Though they were together now, she kept her guard up, just in case. She'd enjoy the sex and their time together until the relationship came to its inevitable end.

"I don't need anyone to take care of me because I make my own money, but I'd like someone who's protective."

She didn't remember her father because he passed when she was only a toddler, so her example of this trait came from Papa Ben. Despite being divorced from her mother, she knew her stepfather would do anything for her. Her care and well-being was of utmost importance to him and as a result, so was the care and wellbeing of her children.

He helped Ethan get started in real estate development, was supportive when Audra became pregnant as a teen, and he was the one who'd taught Monica to ride a bike and how to drive. His patience and care had been a great influence in her life.

"Since you've never found a man with all these qualities, I assume you've never been in love?" Aunt Florence asked.

Monica swallowed. The questions were getting too personal, and she didn't want to answer, particularly since she considered her aunt to be judgmental.

"I haven't found the perfect man," she answered simply.

She'd said *I love you* to Andre. He was the only man to get her to say those words. She'd gone so far as to tattoo her wrist with a permanent reminder of that love. After they split, it reminded her that so-called "love" was fleeting.

"Oh honey, you think love is about the other person and their qualities? Their perfection? If that were the case, everybody would only fall in love with drop dead gorgeous men with big bank accounts and big penises."

"Aunt Florence!"

Her aunt eyed her like someone looking over the rim of glasses. "I was married two times and have four children. I know what the penis is and what it does. I knew long before you were born," she said dryly.

Monica couldn't argue with that.

"A woman who falls in love with a pauper can be happier than a woman living in a mansion with all her needs being met. Do you know why?"

Resting her hands on her hips, Monica braced for the foolishness about to come out of her aunt's mouth. "No, why?"

"Because of the way he makes her feel."

Skeptical, Monica screwed up her face.

"Correct," Aunt Florence said. "I'm talking about the emotion that settles in the pit of your stomach or clogs your throat every time you're near your young man. More than that, I'm talking about what makes us want to be around someone, the love you so desperately want to hide from. It's not because of who he is, but because of how he makes you feel. Who you become when you're together. You're different when you're with him, whether you recognize it or not. There is. No shame. In that. I hope we'll be able to meet him one day." She picked up the *Brides* publication and offered it to Monica.

Monica took the magazine in a daze. As her aunt strolled out of the room, she stared at the happy bride on the front—a queasy sensation in the pit of her stomach.

Chapter Twenty-Five

Something smells good.

Andre closed the door and inhaled the enticing scent of garlic and spices in the air. In his little kitchen, Monica wore an apron and chopped parsley on the cutting board. A few days ago he'd given her a key so she could come and go at will.

"Oh no, you got here before I finished," she said, her bright smile lighting up the room.

Seeing her lifted his spirits after his lousy afternoon.

"How was your day?" Monica asked.

"Didn't go as I'd hoped," he said, launching into an explanation.

Earlier in the week, the first bank he went to turned him down, despite the polished proposal he and Phin prepared. They wanted more collateral. The second bank, which he visited today, also turned him down. They needed him to make a bigger investment before they considered loaning the funds and expressed concern that he was currently unemployed, but he didn't want to put any more money into the deal. He needed to safeguard those funds for his mother's defense.

At this point, he'd been unemployed for a whole month and his stock dividends were negligible compared to the money he used to bring in from the profits at the lounges. He'd wanted to start up the business, but it seemed he might have to find a job first and let the lounge be secondary.

"I'm sorry, baby," Monica said, her eyes filled with sympathy.

Andre shrugged off her concern. "I did get a little good news. I talked to the broker and the property's still available, but I don't know for how much longer."

"You have to think positive. A solution could come out of nowhere, when you least expect it."

Andre managed a smile for the first time in hours. "You always so positive."

"I don't want you to get down. I believe in you."

"Thanks." He leaned over the bar and gave her a quick kiss. "What are you making?"

Monica laughed. "*I* didn't make this. I told Bruno how much you enjoy seafood and asked him to prepare a seafood boil for me. It's got shrimp, sausage, potatoes, the works."

"Smells delicious."

Needing additional contact, he came up behind her and squeezed, bumping his pelvis against her bottom. Monica moaned, and he chuckled, burying his face in the side of her neck.

"You're a bad girl," he whispered.

"Tell me something I don't know," she whispered back.

She puckered her lips, and he kissed the side of her mouth.

"You're going to love this dish. The food is so good. I'm going home on Sunday because the family's getting together, so you have this to eat for the whole weekend while I'm gone."

"Lucky me," he said, though his heart plummeted.

He'd become spoiled having her around all the time. They got up late every morning and drove to a nearby cafe to have breakfast before returning to his apartment where Monica worked virtually with her team. This week she had a photo shoot but was only gone for several hours when she went to her office, which doubled as a creative studio.

"By the way, Phin came by, and I gave him some of the seafood boil."

"He's not supposed come over here without calling first," Andre said.

"He said he tried to call you, but couldn't reach you."

Andre checked his phone and cursed. He saw the missed call from Phin and two other numbers. He'd forgotten to turn the ringer on after he left the meeting at the bank.

Monica turned off the stove. "When he pulled up, he saw my car and knocked. So I let them in."

"Chelle must be out of town again."

"Actually, she's not. He stopped by to say hi, and I offered him some of the food because there's so much. We exchanged numbers so he can call me next time if he can't reach you. He wants the four of us to go on a double date, and I said yes. I hope that's okay?"

"Yeah, should be fun."

"Good."

She spooned a hearty helping of food into a bowl while he washed his hands. Then she sprinkled on chopped parsley.

"Look at you," Andre said.

She laughed. "Don't tease me."

"Looks delicious."

"Thank you," she said almost shyly. He could see she was trying, and he liked seeing her domestic side. "Have a seat."

He sat on a stool while she prepared a helping for herself.

Then she produced a bottle of white wine and handed it to him.

"You do the honors."

He opened the bottle, poured her a generous portion, and fixed himself a rum and Coke. Monica removed crusty bread from the oven, and the aroma of garlic wafted into his nose.

"Don't tell me that's garlic bread."

"It is, and I made it," she said.

Finally, she removed the apron and joined him at the bar. Monica watched him eat, anxiety in her eyes. He made sure to groan his pleasure with the first taste of the seafood and when his teeth crunched into the garlic bread.

"Delicious."

She grinned, picked up her utensils, and started eating.

Later, bellies full, they lounged on the sofa. Monica rested her feet on his lap while he gently massaged her soles.

"Mmm, feels so good." She wiggled her toes. "Oh, I'm going to Miami next week for a couple of days," she said.

"So the deal came through?"

"Yep. They want me to model a bikini from the new line," she said, referring to a swimwear company her team had been negotiating with the past couple of weeks.

Monica asked for certain concessions, and while the company had balked at first, they must have decided she was worth the expense.

"You should come with me."

"Can't. I need to keep pounding the pavement here. I might need to get a job."

"Oh no," she groaned. She knew how much he wanted to get the lounge off the ground.

"Either get a job or put more money into the deal, but if I do put in more money, there's no guarantee the bank will approve my loan, and I won't have much left for my mother's defense."

"Forget your problems for one day and come to Sunday dinner with me. Bruno's cooking a big feast to test out new dishes for one of his restaurants."

"It's not a good idea."

"Why not?"

"I have stuff to do here," Andre said.

Her shoulders drooped. "Sunday is the weekend. Take one day off."

"I can't."

A fine line creased her forehead. "I feel like you don't want to meet my family."

"You're being ridiculous." Andre blew off the accusation by lifting her feet off his lap and going into the kitchen. He poured himself another rum and Coke.

"Then why won't you come to the house? I've asked you before and you always decline. It's obvious there's a problem, so stop denying it."

"And what exactly do you think the problem is?" Andre asked irritably, lifting the glass to his lips.

Monica came to her feet. "I don't know, you tell me."

Andre carefully placed the glass on the bar. "I don't want to argue."

"Why did you break up with me in college? Why didn't you give me a chance to make things right after the incident?"

"This again?"

"Yes, this again, because you never answered the question and I need to know. Is it because of me and my family? Because of the money?"

"No," Andre said with thinly veiled anger.

"Then what's the problem? I don't feel like you're all in.

Why can't you squeeze an hour or two into your busy schedule to spend time with my family? What are we doing?"

"I gave you a key to my place," he pointed out.

"Your cousin has a key to your place. I don't know that it makes me special."

"Again, you're ridiculous."

"I am not. Screw you, Andre!"

He slammed his hands on the counter. "I left Belinda, for you! I lost my job and investments, for you! I took the fall for the drugs—years ago—for you! For you, Monica! Everything I do is for you. Any other man would be considered a simp for his girl, but you're the only woman who would look at our history and think I'm not all in. *I'm not all in.*" He let out a bitter laugh and shook his head in disbelief.

"I didn't ask you to do any of those things."

"Nah, you didn't, but you weren't sorry I did, were you?"

"I appreciate everything you've done. You have done a lot, which is why I don't understand the hesitation to meet my family. They would love you."

He chuckled and swiped up the glass of rum and Coke again. "I'm not so sure about that." He drained the contents in two seconds.

Her brow creased into a frown. "Why are you talking as if you're so sure? My family is not judgmental. They're good people, and I don't appreciate you making that kind of comment."

"You think you know your family so well, don't you? You want to know why I don't want to come to your perfect little Sunday dinner?" He marched over to where she stood and they locked eyes. "Because after the incident at UGA, someone in your family came to my room and warned me away from you."

Her eyes widened.

He hadn't meant to divulge that information, but dammit,

she had gotten him all worked up. Oh well, the truth was out there now.

"No, they didn't."

"Yeah, they did."

"Who?"

"Don't worry about it."

"Tell me who. Was it Ethan?"

"I'm not telling you. Drop it." He shot her a glance meant to shut her up, but a determined Monica was unstoppable.

"I want you to tell me which one of my brothers came to you."

"I'm not going to tell you anything. It was a long time ago and irrelevant. Just know I'm not stepping foot in your family's house without a job or a business so they can look down their nose at me and confirm their assumptions from years ago are true."

The words ricocheted through him with shocking force. Not even to himself had he admitted the real reason he hadn't wanted to meet Monica's family. He didn't want them to see him as lacking. He needed to have something to offer and didn't as an unemployed wannabe entrepreneur.

He started up the stairs and Monica followed him.

"Then their visit is not irrelevant because it still bothers you, and is keeping you from interacting with my family. I want to know who came to you," she said.

He refused to answer, but the words from years ago echoed in his head. *If you love her, you'll leave her alone.*

"They had no right!" He heard the difference in her tear-thickened voice and quickly turned.

Monica blinked rapidly.

Andre cupped her shoulders. "Listen to me, they weren't wrong to warn me away. If I had a daughter dating a man who had been accused of using drugs on campus and got expelled, I'd do the same thing."

"But the drugs were mine."

"It doesn't matter."

"It matters to *me*. You lost everything to protect me, and I want them to know how wonderful you are."

"They will, one day. I need to get my life together. I can't go up in that house with nothing to offer. I can't."

Her eyes brightened. "I could loan you the money."

His hands fell away from her. "I'm not taking money from my woman."

"But—"

"My answer is final." Andre placed a gentle kiss on her forehead and took her hand. "No. I'm doing this on my own."

Her shoulders slumped.

Andre tugged her into his arms.

"Listen to me, I'm good, okay?" he said, rubbing her back. "I didn't want to mention it, but I have a meeting with another bank next week. Based on what they say, I'll put my nose to the grindstone and handle my business so when I meet your family, I can hold my head up."

Monica gazed up at him. "You can hold your head up now. You have nothing to be ashamed of." She flung her arms around his neck and squeezed him tight.

"Monica, I wasn't supposed to tell you about that meeting. Promise me you won't start an argument with your family at Sunday dinner."

She didn't respond.

Didn't even acknowledge he had made the request.

Chapter Twenty-Six

Monica slammed the brakes on her Ferrari and then stormed up the outside steps and into the house. She suspected the family would be eating in the large dining room, but as she marched through the house, she heard masculine laughter in the kitchen and went there first.

She found her two oldest brothers, Bruno and Ethan, laughing about something or the other. The two she wanted to see and start with first.

Bruno was removing a rack of lamb from the industrial size oven, while Ethan relaxed against the counter, ankles crossed as he tossed pumpkin seeds into his mouth.

"Hey, look who finally showed up," Bruno said, placing the roasting pan on top of the stove. "You can help take food out to the terrace."

Monica dropped both hands onto her hips and glowered at her two brothers. "Which one of you told Andre to stay away from me back when I attended UGA?"

Both men spoke at the same time.

"Who?" Bruno asked.

"What?" came from Ethan.

"*Andre Campos,*" Monica said, emphasizing his name. "The guy I was dating back in college who got into trouble for having marijuana on campus. I know one of you said something to him. Ignacio and Thiago wouldn't, and Maxwell was too young to get involved. It had to be one of you."

"Well, you're wrong. At least, it wasn't me," Bruno said, pulling a serving platter from the cabinet.

"Why are you asking about that all of a sudden?" Ethan asked.

The fact that he avoided answering the question made Monica suspicious. Hands still on her hips, she marched over to her older brother and narrowed her eyes.

"Was it you? Did you go to him and warn him away? It's exactly the kind of thing you would do. I want you to admit it."

"Where is this questioning coming from?" Bruno asked.

Monica swung toward him. "Andre and I reconnected, and he told me."

"Back together with a drug dealer?" Ethan said dryly.

"He is not a drug dealer," Monica said.

"If I remember correctly, he didn't have the best background. His mother was in jail, wasn't he?" Bruno asked.

"How dare you judge him!" Monica said.

"I wasn't judging him. I simply pointed out facts, which you seem to want to ignore. Use your brain. Do you really want to get involved with someone like that?"

"It was you, wasn't it? I knew it had to be one out of the two of you, because the two of you think you're my goddamn fathers, and you're not. I am grown, and I was grown then."

Bruno muttered something in Spanish.

"What did you say?"

He repeated the comment in Spanish. "Then act like you're grown instead of acting like a spoiled child."

She shot back a retort in Spanish, and they started arguing, their voices loud and echoing in the kitchen.

"Would the two of you stop," Ethan said, his voice low but commanding.

They ignored him and continued to argue in Spanish, getting into each other's faces.

Ethan stepped between them. "Stop! What is the matter with the two of you?"

Rose rushed into the kitchen. "What is going on in here?" she whispered fiercely. "We can hear you all the way in the great room, and we have company. Benicio invited a couple of friends, and the three of you have completely embarrassed us."

Benicio also entered the kitchen, his face red and angry. "Does anyone care to explain to me what is going on in here?" he asked.

Monica jabbed her finger in the direction of her brothers. "One of them did something unforgivable, but neither of them will admit it. Andre and I are back together, and—"

"What do you mean back together?" Benicio interrupted.

"I mean he and I are seeing each other."

"See, I told you she would get back involved with him," Benicio said, flinging up his hands in despair.

"Is he the young man you've been seeing?" her mother asked. "You told us he was engaged, and there was no interest in getting back together with him."

"He and his fiancée broke up, and he and I are back together." Monica lifted her chin higher. She would not be made to feel guilty or ashamed for spending time with the man she cared about. "As I was saying, he told me something I didn't know before. Someone in the family came to him after he got into trouble with the drugs, and they warned him away from me. One of *them* did it, and I want the guilty party to admit it.

Now." Hands on her hips, she returned her attention to her brothers.

"Neither of them is going to admit it, because it was me," Rose said.

Monica gasped. *"You?"* She couldn't believe it.

Rose clasped her hands in front of her. "He had too much power and influence over you. His behavior was reckless, bringing drugs into your room. He could have gotten you kicked out of school, and worse, hooked on marijuana. I did not raise you to use drugs."

Monica was still in a state of shock. Not once had she considered her mother to be the culprit. In fact, neither Bruno nor Ethan had gone to Andre, she was certain the next likely person was Papa Ben.

"You had no right to do that, Mommy."

"I had every right. You are my daughter, and I will do whatever it takes to protect you. If I had to do it all over again, I would do the same. You had too much to lose, Monica, and I was not going to allow him to have you throw away your life for no reason, the way he had thrown away his."

Monica's eyes burned with unshed tears. "He didn't throw away his life for no reason. He was protecting me. You were wrong. The drugs were mine, and Andre took the blame."

Dead silence filled the kitchen, and Rose's mouth fell open. "What?" she whispered.

"He was the first in his family to go college and had a scholarship, and he lost all of that, because of me." Her voice cracked.

"Oh my goodness." Rose covered her mouth at the same time Benicio placed a hand on her shoulder.

"I won't be joining you all for Sunday dinner. I'm not in the mood anymore."

Monica swept past her parents and hurried down the hall.

She rushed up the stairs, tears of anger and disappointment filling her eyes. Bad enough to learn Andre had broken off their relationship and stayed away because a family member warned him to, but to learn it was her mother, the family member with whom she was the closest, devastated her.

She wished it had been Ethan or Bruno instead. It would still hurt, but there would be no betrayal because she fully expected such behavior from her interfering older siblings.

Upstairs, she lay curled up under the covers, distraught at the turn of events. Poor Andre. He hadn't deserved that.

Staring out the window, she ignored the soft knock on the door. When the door opened, and she glanced over her shoulder to see who had entered.

Rose came and sat on the side of the bed. "I don't know what to say."

Monica sat up. "I trusted you. I cried to you when we broke up."

"I know, but I did what I thought was best."

"All this time, I thought he had broken up with me because I let him take the fall for my actions."

"Monica, I had no idea. I'm not proud of keeping my visit a secret from you, but you also kept a secret from me. Had I known, I wouldn't have gone to him."

"You shouldn't have gone in the first place."

"I am *not* sorry for trying to protect you," Rose said. "I *am* sorry I hurt that young man. I can't imagine what he must have thought."

"I invited him to lunch today, but because of what happened and his current situation, he thinks he's not good enough."

"What's his current situation?"

Reluctantly, Monica explained about her role in Andre and

Belinda's breakup and how that resulted in him losing his job and income stream.

"Oh dear, that's quite a story," Rose said when Monica finished. She covered Monica's hand. "I want you to be happy. If Andre makes you happy—as long as he's not involved in anything illegal..."

"He's not," Monica insisted. Her mother didn't need to know about his recreational drug use.

"What would you like me to do? I could talk to him."

"Would you?" She seized on the offer.

"Gladly. After what he did, the least I can do is thank the young man and let him know he's welcomed here any time."

"That would be perfect." A load lifted off her shoulders, and Monica smiled.

Rose squeezed her hand and then stood. "Now that's settled, you need to come downstairs. You need to apologize too, don't you? You jumped to conclusions about your brothers. Also, Bruno has prepared a feast for all of us, and I'm sure he'd like to have you join us for dinner."

"Okay."

Monica followed her mother out the room.

Chapter Twenty-Seven

Andre's feet pounded the treadmill belt at a high speed. His calves burned and sweat dripped down his face, but he only had two minutes left before the timer went off.

When the chime sounded, he let out a relieved sigh, proud he'd pushed past his limits. He changed the speed into cool down mode and let his heart rate lower. Five minutes later, he mopped sweat from his face and neck on the way to the kitchen for water. He guzzled an entire bottle and was reaching for another when the doorbell chimed.

Who could that be? He wasn't expecting company.

He sauntered over to the door and paused in shock when he saw the woman standing outside. An older woman he immediately recognized as Monica's mother.

He opened the door. "Hello, Mrs. Santana."

"Hello, Andre. I hope I'm not bothering you. May I come in for a few minutes?"

"Yes, sure." He widened the door and allowed her into the apartment. He felt underdressed in black shorts and a blue tank, and he probably smelled after his workout. "If you give me a second, I'll run upstairs and change real quick."

"No need. I won't be long."

Monica's mother walked toward the sofas near the window, and he followed.

"May I?" she asked, gesturing toward one of the sofas.

"Yes, of course."

They sat across from each other.

"Can I get you anything to drink?"

"I'm fine, thank you." She placed a black Chanel tote beside her on the sofa.

He marveled at how Monica was the offspring of this woman, someone petite and soft-spoken compared to her daughter—a tall, outspoken woman who craved the spotlight. Monica had once explained she took after her father in personality and height.

Despite the expensive handbag, Mrs. Santana was dressed simply in low heels, jeans, and a purple blouse. Her hair was piled on top of her head in a curly updo, and she wore a pair of understated diamond earrings in her ears.

She crossed her legs and took a deep breath. "I recently learned I owe you an apology."

Andre frowned. "For what?"

"Monica told me the marijuana the campus police found in her room did not belong to you, but you took the blame."

Sighing, Andre sat back in the chair. "She shouldn't have told you that. Did she make a scene?"

"You know my daughter."

They shared a knowing laugh.

"I'm sorry, Mrs. Santana. I know we agreed our conversation would remain between us. I shouldn't have said anything. Monica and I got into a fight, and it slipped out."

"You have nothing to be sorry for." She smiled in a kind,

motherly way. "I like to think I'm close with my children, and they can come to me with anything. It hurt that she kept the truth about her drug use and what you did from me, but I hurt her when she found out what I did. It also upset me that I blamed you, when in fact Monica was the one who had engaged in illegal activity. Obviously, as her mother, I was disappointed to learn this bit of information. Why didn't you say anything when I came to you?"

Andre shrugged. "Didn't matter, and maybe... maybe you were right, despite the truth of the circumstances. I wasn't the right man for Monica. I'd done things I wasn't proud of in my past. Besides, I smoked weed with her, so I wasn't completely innocent. Truthfully, I was still working on me. In an odd way, getting in trouble helped keep me straight and made me work harder for what I wanted."

She studied him for a moment. "I hope you're not saying that to absolve me of guilt."

"No, it's the truth."

She intertwined her fingers on her knee. "I'm glad you got a lesson out of the experience. Nonetheless, I'm very sorry for the things I said to you, for discouraging you from seeing my daughter, and I hope you can forgive me."

Andre couldn't believe this woman sat across from him asking for forgiveness. "Mrs. Santana, there's nothing to forgive. You did what any mother would have done with the information you had."

"Please, call me Rose. You're very kind and understanding. Much kinder than I deserve. Monica said you declined her invitation to Sunday dinner, but I hope you'll join us at the next get together."

"I would love to. Thank you."

"Good." She picked up her handbag and stood. "Do you care about my daughter, Andre?"

"I care about her a lot."

"Then don't be a stranger. I know Monica can be a handful, but I hope you're confident enough and strong enough to handle such a strong personality. She's worth it."

"I couldn't agree more."

She smiled and made her way to the door but paused before stepping out. "One of my sons, Bruno, is having a party on Saturday night. He made some renovations to his house and invited us over to see the changes. He's cooking, and since he's a chef, expect the food to be delicious. Monica will be back from Miami by then. Would you like to join us?"

"I'd love to."

She beamed a smile at him. "I'm happy to hear that. I'll make sure Monica invites you on Friday. Have a good day."

He watched her get into a chauffeur-driven town car and then closed the door.

Andre dialed Monica's number right away. "Hey, Sunshine, where are you?"

"On my way to the airport."

"I guess you know why I'm calling."

"I have an idea," she said in a guarded tone.

"I had a very interesting conversation with your mother." He paced the floor while talking.

"And...?"

"I should be upset with you. I told you not to say anything."

"But you're not upset, right?"

Andre dropped onto the sofa. He couldn't stay mad at her. "No, I'm not. I'm glad we got everything straightened out. She invited me to your brother Bruno's place on Friday."

"Yay! You'll get to meet everybody. Well, everybody who's available."

She sounded so excited, he couldn't help but smile.

"I miss you. When are you coming back?"

"Wednesday. Oh, I'm sending Daisy to pick up a dress I forgot needs to go to the cleaners. She should be there pretty soon."

"She's not going with you to Miami?"

"Not this time."

"All right. I'll take a quick shower before she gets here."

"I can't wait until Friday!" Monica let out a high-pitched squeal.

Andre dropped his voice. "I can't wait till Wednesday when you're back in town."

"Oh yeah? Why?" Monica asked in a hushed whisper.

They spent the next few minutes talking dirty to each other until Monica had to end the call. Andre hauled the sweaty blue tank over his head and was heading for the staircase when the doorbell rang.

"Damn," he muttered, hoping Daisy hadn't already arrived. Unfortunately, when he checked the peephole, it was her.

He swung open the door. "Hey."

She blinked and stared at his bare chest. "Oh. Hi."

Andre cursed under his breath. "My bad. I was about to take a shower." He unwound the crumpled tank in his hand and slipped his head and arms through the openings. "Come on in."

"Thanks. Monica sent me to pick up a few things for her." Daisy stepped into the apartment.

In the short time he'd known her, Daisy had really stepped her game up fashion wise and seemed to have lost weight. She was almost the same size as Monica. She had multiple piercings in her right ear, wore makeup, and her outfits were often by top designers, including today's ensemble of dark jeans, a gold halter top, and Mignonne espadrilles.

Did Monica notice the similarities?

"I was talking to her a few minutes ago. You know what you're looking for?" Andre asked.

"Yes. They should be in the closet."

"They? She said you were picking up a dress."

"I'm also getting the accessories, because I'm sure she'll need them. If I don't, I'll have to make another trip over here when she thinks about it." She rolled her eyes.

Andre chuckled. "What would she do without you?"

"Hopefully, she'll never have to know."

They laughed together. He led the way up the stairs and pulled across the frosted glass door leading to his bedroom.

"I really liked this set up when I first saw it. Such a unique design," Daisy said, following him inside.

"The design is why I ended up renting this place, and the apartment's proximity to downtown. I lucked out by getting in when rents were low. They're almost double what I pay now."

"Oh, I bet. Housing is getting so expensive everywhere." She wrinkled her nose. "Do you mind if I ask you something?"

"No, I don't mind."

"I've never seen the tattoo on your chest before. What do the stars mean?"

He explained the meaning to her.

"That's beautiful."

"My grandfather was a wise man. I remembered his words, and the tattoo is a way for me to always remember to do what he said—aim high and pursue my dreams, no matter what."

"And these." Her fingers traced the skin of his forearm.

In the small room, all alone, her touch made him uncomfortable, and he moved back a step. Was her touch innocent or something more?

"That's my father's name in clouds," he explained, about the tattoo on the side of his left forearm. He quickly explained the tiger, the snake wrapped around his arm, and the other images. When he finished, he asked, "Did you want to go ahead and get the dress?"

"Oh! I almost forgot why I came." She grinned.

She retrieved an elegant black number with a gold design and picked up shoes and a few accessories from Monica's drawer.

"I think that's it," she said, with the dress draped over her arm and the accessories in hand.

"Okay." Andre waited for her to leave, but she just stood there. "You have a question or...?"

"Monica is very, very lucky to have a man like you. She can trust you."

"Thanks," he said, his discomfort expanding. What a strange thing to say.

Daisy left the room, and Andre followed down the stairs.

"Bye," she called cheerily, going out the door.

The moment she left, Andre locked the door, hoping his unease was ill-placed.

Chapter Twenty-Eight

Bruno Santana's main home—Monica explained he owned other residences around the country—was a large one-story on a basement to the north of the city. When Andre drove the Escalade up the long driveway, the park pad was already filled with the high-end cars of family members. He parked behind a limousine and climbed out of the SUV with a small charcuterie board in hand.

Monica told him that he didn't need to bring food or a gift, but he couldn't justify showing up empty-handed. Passing by her yellow Ferrari, bright lights bombarded him from the windows all the way to the double front doors. The doors were basically glass in wood frames, which allowed him to see inside the house as he approached.

Monica raced to open the door in a silver peasant dress—a little mini she wore off her shoulders and accessorized with a pair of silver chandelier earrings. With her long legs on display and her dark skin glowing, she looked absolutely breathtaking.

She yanked open the door.

"Hey!" She flung herself into his arms, as if months had

passed since they last saw each other, and she hadn't seen him this morning, right before she left his apartment.

He squeezed her with one arm because the other hand held the board. Kissing her firmly on the mouth, he let his tongue briefly touch hers but resisted the urge to linger and grab her ass. Fortunately so, since her mother and a tall man with black hair and gray eyes suddenly came out of nowhere.

Grabbing his hand like she would never let him go, Monica led Andre to them.

"Hello, Andre, I'm happy you could join us," Rose said. "Bruno, this is Andre, Monica's boyfriend."

"Welcome to my home." Bruno extended his hand, and Andre shifted the charcuterie board to the other hand for the handshake.

"Nice to meet you. Monica told me not to bring anything, but I brought a little something anyway. The woman at the deli said I couldn't go wrong with this particular platter."

"How thoughtful of you. It's a fine accompaniment to the menu. I'll place it on the table outside with the hors d'oeuvres," Rose said.

"Thank you, Andre. Did you find the house okay?" Bruno asked.

"I did. The GPS brought me straight to you with no problem."

"Excellent. Come on, let me show you into the kitchen, which received most of the renovations. The contractors also did work on the outside, which you'll see later," Bruno said.

Monica locked hands with Andre, grinning up at him, so happy and excited, he regretted not visiting with her family before. Better late than never.

There was a flurry of activity in the kitchen, a bright, spacious room that sparkled under the overhead lights with shiny new appliances. A huge island in the middle contained platters of food in the midst of being prepped by a man and woman dressed in a uniform of white shirts and black pants.

"This is my domain," Bruno said proudly, spreading his hands wide. "I've wanted to renovate the house for years, but my busy schedule always kept me from doing it. I finally decided there might never be a right time, so I started the renovations while I worked on my restaurant in Las Vegas and communicated with the contractors on FaceTime. Not ideal and very stressful."

"Then they ran behind," Monica added, plucking a green olive from one of the platters and popping it in her mouth.

"Whenever there are renovations, there are always delays. I learned the hard way working in restaurant industry."

"I don't think we ever hit a deadline on renovations at any of the clubs and lounges where I worked over the years," Andre said.

"So you know what I'm talking about," Bruno said.

A little girl whom he guessed was seven or eight elbowed her way between Bruno and Andre.

Gazing up at him, she said, "Hi, I'm Tracy."

Andre grinned down at her. "Hi Tracy, I'm Andre."

"Tracy is Audra's daughter. This is my friend I was telling you about," Monica told the little girl.

Before Andre could respond, an older gentleman with gray hair on his head and face came into the kitchen. He introduced himself as Benicio Santana, which Andre had already guessed.

"Monica tells me you have Nicaraguan roots," he said, in accented English.

"Yes. On my father's side."

Benicio lapsed into Spanish, and although Andre understood most of what he said, he had a hard time responding. He explained as much in halting Spanish.

Benicio return to English. "Monica can help you with that. She speaks fluent Spanish."

Andre relaxed, appreciative of Benicio's nonjudgmental, welcoming nature. "I'll have to make her practice with me."

"Do you want to see the watchtower?" Tracy interrupted. She had remained in the midst of the adult conversation.

"The watchtower?" Andre repeated.

Monica responded. "It's easy to miss from the front of the house, but Bruno built a watchtower we can access from inside. It's magical. Right, Tracy?" Monica tweaked her niece's nose.

The little girl agreed with a giggle and vigorous nod.

"It was a bit of a vanity project," Bruno admitted with a laugh. "You can see the entire neighborhood from up there. Because my house is outside the city limits, it's a great place to star gaze. I have a telescope up there."

"Want to see it?" Monica asked.

"Sure," Andre said.

"Yay! Come." Tracy tugged him out of the kitchen.

Andre allowed the little girl to draw him deeper into the house. They went through a door he thought was a closet, but instead led to a winding metal staircase. Tracy raced up ahead of them.

"Take your time," Monica warned.

She climbed the stairs with greater care than her niece. From the angle below her, Andre had a nice view. Her bare ass and thong flashed him under the short dress.

He pinched her left butt cheek, and she swatted away his hand, which made him chuckle.

Three stories up, they reached the top of the staircase, and Tracy pushed open a door in the ceiling which led to the watchtower.

A little boy who appeared close in age to Tracy glanced at them.

"Hi," he said.

Monica introduced them, and Andre learned the boy's name was Damon, Junior, Tracy's older brother.

While Junioor returned his attention to peering through the telescope angled at the black starry sky, Monica closed the door in the floor.

"Isn't this cool?" she asked.

"You can see everything from up here." Andre gazed at the spattering of other homes in the area and the city lights in the distance.

"It's so tranquil up here. I love it," Monica said.

Her niece tugged on her dress. "Auntie, what does tranquil mean?"

"It means calm and peaceful. Do you agree?"

Tracy nodded.

Monica clearly had a good relationship with the little girl, and Tracy stuck close to her side. The way they interacted conjured thoughts of Monica with a one or two kids of her own —*their* kids.

An engine roared nearby, and a red Corvette came tearing up the long driveway.

"Ignacio, making a scene as usual," Monica said.

He still couldn't believe Ignacio Santana was her stepbrother. The guy was an A-list actor whose last movie earned him a cool $15 million salary and back end residuals. Before his last blockbuster hit, he tried his hand at directing a small film, which critics panned and which received mixed reviews from the general public. Andre wondered if he would try his hand at directing again or stick to acting.

Ignacio screeched to a stop behind Andre's Escalade. Seconds later he exited the car, hair tied back in a curly ponytail.

"Why do you always have to show off?" Monica yelled down at him.

"Hi, Uncle Ignacio," the kids yelled, waving.

Ignacio didn't respond to Monica's remark, but from their position, Andre saw he was smiling. He waved at the kids before disappearing below the line of the rooftop.

"We better go. It's probably time to start eating now that Mr. Movie Star has arrived. Come on, kids."

They made their way downstairs and out to the back of the property, where lights strewn across the pergola created a welcoming picture and enhanced the beauty of the outdoor space. The outdoor kitchen and dining area included a large grill and pizza oven. From the newness of the exterior extras, this must be the renovations Bruno had mentioned.

With a few more introductions, Andre met Thiago, Audra, her oldest daughter, and the eldest son, Ethan and his fiancée, Skye.

"Auntie Monica, can I sit with you?" Tracy took Monica's hand.

"Yes, you can, sweet pea," Monica said.

"I'll sit next to *you*," Rose said to Andre, her smile gentle.

She sat to his left, Monica sat to his right, and Tracy sat to her right. Bruno and his father took places at either end of the long table, which turned out to be two tables pushed together end to end.

Once everyone was seated, Benicio stood and looked down the table at his gathered family. "Everyone is here, yes?"

"Except Maxwell," Monica said.

A series of moans filled the table.

"And me," a male voice said.

Everyone turned in the direction of the open doorway.

"Daddy!" Tracy screamed.

204

Damon stopped next to Bruno's chair, holding a bottle of wine in a wine bag. "Looks like I got here just in time."

A chorus of excited chatter started. Clearly, the family hadn't seen him in a while. He smiled and nodded at the welcoming chorus of voices, but Andre noticed his wife was the only person who didn't express the same excitement as the rest of the family.

As Damon pulled a chair to the table, Andre leaned toward Monica. "How did I not know Damon Foster is your brother-in-law?"

Damon used to play professional baseball and spent his last three years with the Atlanta Braves before retiring at the height of his career.

"Did I not mention that?" she asked.

"Nah, you didn't mention that. Half your family is famous. Anybody else I need to know about?"

She laughed and rubbed her shoulder against his. He wished he could dip his lips to her soft skin.

"Last famous person, I promise," Monica said.

After Damon settled in a chair across from his wife, Benicio said a brief prayer to bless the food, and then everyone started to eat.

Chapter Twenty-Nine

Belly full of tender steak and roasted duck accompanied by a plethora of sides, Andre chilled on one of the outdoor sofas across from Ethan and his fiancée, talking about Ethan's mixed-use development, Horizon, and Skye's work at a community learning center.

Monica's oldest brother was an interesting guy. Though dressed casually in a navy polo shirt and black slacks, Andre had the distinct impression this man didn't often do casual. His eyes remained observant even when he laughed and chatted with family members. His fiancée seemed to be the perfect foil to his quiet bearing, sitting with her feet curled beside her on the cushion, one arm wrapped around Ethan's as she leaned against him.

Andre couldn't help but notice the massive yellow diamond on her finger. The thing must have cost a small fortune but was nothing for these people. They were all obviously doing well financially, but he didn't feel as out of place as he thought he would.

He had planned to leave right after dinner if he didn't get a good vibe from Monica's family, but after more than two hours expected to stay as long as everyone else hung around.

The Connor-Santanas were a down to Earth, friendly group, welcoming him by drawing him into conversations and asking questions about his family and background. He answered candidly, but none of his answers seemed to surprise them. He figured Monica must have already given them a summary of his mother's situation, and though they didn't speak about the incident that caused him to get kicked out of UGA years ago, he sensed the adults were well aware of what had occurred.

Audra approached from behind Ethan and Skye. Resting her hand on the back of the chair, she leaned over and said to Skye, "You have to come see this. It's the episode of *Say Yes to the Dress* I was telling you about."

"Oh, I wanted to see that."

Skye shot up from the chair, and the two women hurried inside, leaving Andre and Ethan alone.

When Andre had walked through the house earlier, family members congregated in small groups. In the game room Bruno and his father played an intense chess game, while the kids played old school arcade games.

"What's *Say Yes to the Dress?*" Andre asked.

"It's a show about women buying wedding dresses."

"That's it? They show women buying dresses?"

"More or less. It's a reality show about a bridal shop in Manhattan."

"Smart way to advertise," Andre said.

"Brilliant." Ethan picked up his glass of iced tea and glanced over at the table where raucous laughter came from Damon, Thiago, and Ignacio. "Do you have a minute? I wanted to talk to you in private."

Great. Here it comes.

He should have known the perfect night was too good to be true. Monica had told him about her protective brother, so he imagined this was the part where Ethan gave him some kind of warning. Monica was a grown woman of thirty, and besides, he would never hurt her. He'd listen to Ethan and then speak his peace.

"Sure."

"Let's step over here for a minute." Ethan led him onto the lawn, away from the outdoor lights and the other men.

"I'm sure you're wondering what this is about."

"I am."

Ethan swirled his tea, and the ice clinked against the tall glass. "Monica told me you're unemployed. She mentioned skills and experience in the hospitality industry, and I checked into your background."

"I don't know why Monica did that. I never asked her to come to you about anything."

Ethan waved away the comment. "I know. Don't worry, she's made me very aware you have no interest in getting help from anyone."

The comment sounded like a dig, and Andre straightened his spine. "That's right. I'll find a solution to my problem. Done it before, and I'll do it again, so if you pulled me aside to offer a position with your company, I'll have to respectfully decline."

He did not want to be in another unsavory situation like when his relationship with Belinda fell apart—beholden to a family member of the woman he dated.

"I didn't ask to speak to you to offer you a position," Ethan said in flat tone.

Andre relaxed, but now he was confused about the reason for this side conversation. "So why did you want to talk to me?"

"I wanted to give you some advice. Before I begin, do you know how I got started in real estate?"

"Vaguely."

"My stepfather, Benicio. When I graduated from high school, he bought a rundown property and gave it to me as a graduation gift. The place looked like crap. I wanted a car, but after some thought, I accepted the property. He allowed me to finance the renovations through him. With his guidance, by the end of the summer, *before* I started college, I had an income-producing property, and my first taste of what real estate could do. I was hooked. I said all that to say, very few people have 'made it' on their own, so if you think it makes you any less of a man because you accept help, get rid of that notion right away. You're only stunting your growth potential."

Andre didn't respond immediately. Knee-jerk reaction, he wanted to tell Ethan to shove his advice. He didn't need a practical stranger telling him what to do. He was a grown ass man and *knew* what to do. Hustle harder and find his way out of the hole.

Then, he calmed down and marinated on the words. This man had made it to the top of the real estate field, a multi-billionaire in his thirties because someone else helped him.

"I hear you, but when people help, they make it known you owe them, and when they give, they can take away."

"Sure, in the specific circumstance with Chambers Enterprises—Monica told me all about it—you ended up losing your job and investment income, but Chambers can't take away the experience you gained any more than my stepfather could take away my experience or the property I owned outright. My point is, because of the chance Nigel gave you, you have experience you can take elsewhere, correct?"

"Yeah," Andre said with a shrug.

"Which brings me to the second reason I wanted to talk to you. I said I don't have a job to offer, but I do have an offer for you."

Andre's neck tightened with discomfort. "Listen—"

"Hear me out." Ethan lifted his hand to stop him from talking. "I took a look at the property you want to turn into a lounge and the neighborhood. Based on my experience, if you get your hands on that warehouse, you'll be in a prime location to grow your business as well as own a piece of real estate that could greatly increase in value over time. It's not going to last much longer before sharks like me swoop in and buy up everything in the area."

He was right, which had been Andre's concern for some time. He considered himself fortunate it hadn't happened yet.

"If you're as interested in the location as Monica says you are, I'll buy it and you can purchase it from me. I'll also finance the renovations."

Stunned, Andre couldn't believe what he was hearing. "Are you serious?"

"Yes."

"You barely know me. Why?"

Granted, the cost of the building and financing the renovations would be a negligible about for a man with his wealth, but his calculations estimated the total cost at close to a million dollars, and Andre was more or less a stranger.

"Monica asked me to." Ethan drank some of his tea. "But let me make something clear, I don't do anything I don't want to. My sister asked, but I did my due diligence and researched you. I've helped out people before, mostly family members, and they've burned me. I do my best not to make the same mistake twice. If you're not interested and not willing to do the work, I need to know. If you screw up, I *will* take that building and make money off of it."

Andre had his pride, but he was no fool. "I'm interested."

"Good. I'll need your business plan. Monica said you have

one? Oh, and I have one more requirement before I offer you the loan."

Andre groaned inwardly. Of course, a catch.

His expression must have given away his thoughts. Ethan looked amused.

"You don't trust easily, do you?" he asked.

"No, I don't."

"The requirement is, you have to work toward the completion of your degree in hospitality management."

Andre rested in silent confusion for a moment. "That's it?"

"Yes. Do you think you can handle going to school and opening a business?"

"I wouldn't be the first to do it."

Ethan nodded, approving of the answer. He couldn't be more than five or six years older than Andre, but he had the air of someone much older.

"As soon as you get me your business plan, I'll have my attorney draw up the contract for us to sign. Monica has my work email address. Send the proposal there. It was good talking to you."

Ethan extended his hand, and Andre shook it.

"Likewise. I don't know what to say, except thanks."

"Don't thank me yet. I need to see your plan."

"I'll have it for you by Monday." He would spend the weekend reviewing every single detail before he emailed the proposal.

Ethan strolled over to the table where his brothers and brother-in-law sat in conversation.

In a daze, Andre didn't move for a while. *Holy. Shit.* He was going to get the property and a construction loan to fix it up to his own specs. His dream was about to come true. If his planned down payment satisfied Ethan, he could keep the extra funds he needed to make sure his mother's attorneys got paid.

Everything was falling into place. He was happy enough to howl at the moon. Instead, he went in search of Monica and found her in the kitchen munching on leftovers while scrolling Instagram.

"Hey," she said.

Without a word, he bent her over his arm and gave her a long, thorough kiss. When he finally let her up for air, her chestnut eyes sparkled with surprise and desire.

She clutched her chest. "What was that for?"

"For being you." He then grabbed Monica's hand and dragged her out the room and into the hall bathroom.

She giggled as he locked the door. "Now?" she asked, sounding excited.

"I don't want to have sex, you little freak."

Monica pouted.

Andre pushed her against the counter with a laugh and rested his hands on her slim hips. "Well, maybe in a minute. I talked to Ethan."

Her eyes doubled in size. "And...?"

"I should be mad at you for telling my business."

She shot him a coquettish look. "But...?"

"I forgive you, and... thank you. I accepted his offer."

"Yes!"

They kissed, mouths traveling hungrily over each other before they stopped.

"I told him about the place, he checked it out and said right away it was a good deal."

"He did a background check on me too, apparently."

"Well, my brother's no fool. Baby, I'm so happy. And you're really not mad?"

"I'm not mad. He did mention that as a condition of the loan, I have to work on finishing my degree, though."

"Oh no. I mentioned you didn't graduate, but I never told him to do anything like that."

"It's all good. It's going to take me a while because I'll only be able to go part-time, but I'm going to make sure it's done. Then I'll frame my diploma, and when my mom gets out of prison, I'm handing it to her."

"She'll be so proud," Monica whispered.

His voice lowered. "Couldn't have done it without my Sunshine."

He kissed her again, this time softer, tasting the sweetness of her mouth and then pressed his lips to her exposed shoulder. Finally. Her damn shoulders had been tempting him all night.

"Think we have time for a quickie?" he asked huskily, kissing his way up her neck.

"I think so," Monica whispered breathlessly.

He shoved her thong past her hips, and Monica stepped out of the scrap of lace and hopped up on the counter.

"I like this dress," Andre murmured, gliding his hands up her outer thighs as she slid the zipper down the bulge in his pants. "I like every dress you wear."

"How much do you like this one?"

"A helluva lot."

He slipped on a condom and pulled her to the edge of the counter. She was already wet, so he easily sank in. Monica whimper-moaned—a sexy sound unique to her that made the hairs on his neck pop straighten—and he lifted her knees higher.

She bit her lip to avoid crying out when Andre thrust deep, her warm, wet core, intoxicating his senses and heightening his hunger.

Breathing hard, he rested his forehead against hers. "You're so damn sexy. So fucking sweet. I love you so much," he whispered.

The minute the words slipped out, they both froze.

Andre saw wide-eyed panic in her eyes but experienced a sense of peace. His love for Monica was all encompassing and brought him happiness. He wanted to offer the same peace of mind to her that she did for him but saw right away she wasn't ready for the deeper, more meaningful shift in their relationship. He loved her so much he didn't care and was willing to wait until she was ready.

"Andre, I..."

"Shh. I want you to know I love you, and that's all that matters right now. I know how you feel."

He gently kissed her mouth and the inside of her wrist where the intertwined hearts—the original symbol of their undying love for one another—was etched into her skin. Though she didn't say the words, he knew the truth.

"Forever with you ain't enough," he said, his voice raw with emotion.

She gripped the back of his head and kissed him harder. His dick throbbed, and he grabbed her hips, driving into her over and over until they both shuddered through a bone-melting climax.

Chapter Thirty

Andre and Phin sat at the kitchen bar with the laptop open and printed copies of the business plan spread out before them. Chelle lounged on one of the sofas behind them, occupied by watching TV while they worked.

"What do you think?" Andre asked.

He and his cousin had reviewed the numbers and tweaked a few sentences in the plan, but otherwise believed it to be sound.

"This is as good as it's going to be, unless he wants something else," Phin replied.

"Okay, time to send it."

Andre saved the file and attached it, hitting Send to the email address Monica gave him last night.

Phin let out a sigh and clutched his chest. "Man, I'm kinda nervous. We're so close."

Andre clapped his cousin on the back to ease his concern. "We're good. It's going to happen."

"When is Ethan supposed to get back to you?" Phin asked.

"He didn't say. I'm hoping within a couple of days we'll have the loan and can get started."

"Did he tell you about the terms?"

"I don't know shit except this man said he's loaning me the money."

Phin laughed. "Can't be predatory though, right? Monica's his sister. Hopefully he wouldn't screw over her boyfriend, but you never know. I'ma keep it positive. We 'bout to be in business, baby! Chelle, you hear that?"

He hopped off the stool, and Chelle muted the television.

"I heard you. You'll be going back to work, finally. Do you remember what work is?" Chelle, light-skinned with dark eyes and cherry-red wavy hair, shot a teasing glance at Phin.

"Vaguely. It's what peasants do, right?"

She laughed, shaking her head. "You are so silly."

Phin rushed over to the sofa and gave her a loud kiss on the neck. She giggled, falling backward as he climbed on top of her.

"I need the two of you to take all that lovey-dovey shit to your own apartment, please," Andre said.

"I'm sorry, Dre." Chelle pushed Phin off her and straightened her blouse. "I meant to ask you earlier, where is Monica tonight?"

"At an industry party for influencers. She's coming by later."

"You didn't want to go?"

"It wasn't that kind of party. The invitation was strictly for influencers, no plus one, and offered an exclusive tasting experience for a new vodka. She's not sure she wants to promote the brand but likes going to events for the networking opportunities. She'll probably leave with a bottle or two of free liquor."

"Must be nice," Phin said.

"You wouldn't believe the amount of free stuff she gets. It's ridiculous."

Phin stood with a groan and extended a hand to Chelle, helping her off the sofa. "We 'bout to leave and get out of your hair. Let me know as soon as you hear something from Monica's brother."

"I will."

Chelle tucked her leather purse—the new one Phin had purchased, over her shoulder. Andre had to admit, his cousin had done good choosing the stylishly elegant bag.

The doorbell sounded, and he frowned. Monica had a key, so that couldn't be her arriving early.

"You expecting company?" Phin asked.

"Nobody but Monica, but later."

He went to the door, surprised when he saw Daisy standing outside. "It's Daisy." He opened the door.

She smiled brightly at the three of them. "Hi, thank goodness you're here. I was nearby when I got a flat. I drove really slowly over here because I need your help. I don't know how to change a tire."

She wore skintight jeans and an unbuttoned short-sleeved sweater over a white tank top squeezing her bosom so tight, her breasts overflowed the top.

"You got a flat, huh? Lucky you were close by." Phin sounded all suspicious as he glanced at Andre.

Andre wanted to kick him in the shin for thinking something might be going on between him and Daisy.

"You two are leaving?" Daisy asked.

"Yeah, we're on our way home." Phin cast one last glance at Andre, who glared at him this time.

"Bye," Daisy said, waving at his cousin and his girlfriend.

After they left, Andre said, "Let's take a look at your car."

She had parked her Nissan Altima right out front in an empty parking space.

He immediately noticed the flat tire at the front passenger side.

"What happened?" Andre bent and examined the damage.

"I have no idea. I must've run over a nail or something."

He straightened. "You have all the tools?"

"Yes." Daisy popped the trunk, and he removed the jack and the doughnut wheel.

She lingered off to the side while he worked.

"I feel so helpless. Is there anything I can do?"

"Nah, you good. I'll have you straight in a few minutes." He began jacking up the car.

"I talked to Monica, and she said you met her family on Friday night. You went to Bruno's?"

"Yeah. He has a nice place with a watchtower for stargazing. The kitchen is beautiful, of course."

"Of course. You'd think he would get tired of cooking, but he loves it. How was the food?"

Andre finished jacking up the car and started on the lug nuts. "Delicious. He served steaks and roast duck and had a bunch of sides—wild rice, potatoes, different vegetables. A lot of food." He and Monica left with enough leftovers to eat well for a couple of days.

"Did you say roast duck? I don't think I've ever had duck before."

"It's not something I eat often myself, but man, it was good."

"So I guess you're in with the family now?"

Andre paused and glanced up at her. That was an odd question. "I don't know about all that." He placed the second lug nut on the ground beside him.

"Of course you are. Monica and her family are very sweet and kind. They make you feel welcomed, and Monica—well, she has such an outgoing personality."

"She does." Andres struggled with one of the nuts, and put a little extra muscle into the turn, finally able to loosen it with a grunt and hard twist.

"I barely see her anymore, though."

"What do you mean?"

"She's always so busy. For instance, this week the trip to Miami and then Friday night, the dinner at her brother's. I haven't seen her all week, if you can believe that. Then tonight she's coming here to spend time with you, instead of going home. We don't hang out like we used to. She no longer needs me."

Andre shot a look in her direction. "Of course she needs you. You're her right hand person."

"Doesn't feel that way anymore. I guess should find other ways to occupy my time."

Her voice dropped low at the end, and the unease from the last time they interacted alone came back. The comment presented a minefield he didn't want to cross, so he simply removed the busted tire.

"Do you mind if I use your restroom real quick?"

"Nah, go ahead. You know where it is, right?"

"On the other side of the sofas?"

"Right."

"Be right back."

Andre watched her enter the apartment. He didn't know what to think about Daisy. Mostly, she seemed sweet, but coming by here unannounced with a flat tire and talking about finding other ways to occupy her time made him suspicious. He could say something to Monica, but what would he say? She hadn't actually done anything.

He continued to work, and by the time he tightened the last nut, she returned from inside.

"Oh my goodness, thank you so much! You're a lifesaver."

"You're welcome."

"I should pay you."

"Don't be ridiculous." Andre placed the bad tire and the tools in her trunk. "You know to buy a new tire right away, right? They might even be able to patch this one for you."

"I know, and I'll take care of it first thing in the morning. You sure I can't pay you?"

"Absolutely not necessary."

"I'll be sure to put in a good word for you with Monica."

She laughed, but he got the impression she wasn't really trying to be funny.

"Good night," Daisy said.

He watched her back out of the parking space. She was definitely an odd one.

He shook off his uncomfortable feeling and went inside.

* * *

Andre wrapped his arms around Monica and squeezed, lifting her off the ground. It was crazy to think how much he missed her when they were apart.

"How was it?"

"Informative. Interesting. Entertaining."

"Are you going to work with them?" he asked.

"Thinking about it." She lifted a bottle of vodka from the cloth bag branded with the company's logo. "Try it and tell me what you think."

"Not tonight. I'm exhausted. I need to sleep." He placed the vodka on the kitchen bar and took her hand, leading the way upstairs.

"Did you and Phin finish working on the business plan?"

"Yes. It's in your brother's hands now."

"He wants to work with you, so if the plan isn't exactly

what he's looking for, he'll let you know so you can fix it. Trust me. He's a big softy."

"I'll have to trust you because nothing about him said softy to me," Andre said, sliding across the door to his bedroom.

They undressed, Andre remaining in his boxers while Monica pulled on one of his gray T-shirts. He slipped under the covers, and she crawled in with him.

Monica moaned. "I think this bed is my favorite place in the whole world."

"Good news for me."

They kissed tenderly, and he gazed into her eyes. "I miss you like crazy when we're not together."

"Same," she said softly.

Andre kissed her forehead the bridge of her nose, and then the tip of her nose. A contented smile tipped up the corners of her mouth, and she snuggled closer to him.

He shifted and something—an article of clothing—tangled around his toes.

"What the heck...?" he asked.

"What's wrong?"

Andre dipped under the covers and retrieved a purple lace thong.

"Used underwear goes in the hamper, madam." He twirled the underwear on one finger.

Monica's face remained unsmiling. "That's not mine."

He laughed. "Well it ain't mine."

Monica sat up. "I'm serious, that's not my thong. Whose is it?"

Andre stopped twirling, awash in a sense of dread.

Chapter Thirty-One

Monica scrambled out the bed and slammed her hands on her hips. "*Whose is it?*"

Andre climbed out the bed but left the thong on the covers. "It has to be yours."

"I'm telling you it's not. Did you have another woman in here?"

"Of course not!"

"Then where did *that* come from?" She jabbed her finger at the thong.

"I have no idea. I don't know whose fucking panties those are."

"And *that* is the problem."

They stared at each other—she with anger and he with what she considered to be faux innocence and shock.

Andre ran his hands down his face in exasperation. "Monica, come on, you really think I would do this to you? You were here last night."

"You had the whole day to yourself, to hook up with

whoever the owner of those panties are." How could he do this, especially after he said he loved her only two days ago!

"I would never dip out on you."

"Never?"

His features tightened. "I never fucked you while Belinda and I were together."

"You wanted to, but we were interrupted twice. I don't know if I can trust you."

"Well then I don't know if I can trust *you*. I had a woman but my relationship status didn't matter to you." He muttered a low curse. "Our situation is different, and you know it."

"I don't know anything. All I know is that we found a pair of panties in your bed, and they don't belong to me." Her voice shook, disbelief and hurt overtaking her emotions and landing blow after blow to her heart. "Tell me how they got there."

Andre's shoulder's sagged. The forlorn expression on his face tugged at her heart, but she didn't know what to believe.

"Monica, baby, I don't know how they got there. I swear. If I knew, I would—" His lips tightened as he growled low in his throat. "Daisy."

"They're Daisy's?" Monica screeched.

"No!" Andre answered quickly. "Well, maybe, but not in the way you think. She came by earlier, said she had a flat tire. While I changed the tire, she came into the apartment to use the restroom."

"You're really suggesting Daisy left one of her panties in your bed?"

"Maybe not *her* panties, but they belong to someone. She planted them. Had to be her."

"Daisy is my employee. More importantly, she's my friend. Why would she do that?"

Andre muttered another curse. "I wasn't sure if I should say anything, but she's been acting weird around me. I think she might be interested in me. The whole flat-tire thing was suspicious. She just happened to have a flat right near my apartment? And the way she was dressed..." He shook his head.

"How was she dressed?" Monica asked, narrowing her eyes.

"Don't do that."

"How was she dressed, Andre? You noticed, so her outfit must have been noteworthy."

Rough, mirthless laughter left his lips. "A'ight, she wore tight jeans and a tank top that didn't hide much. Her breasts were practically coming out of the top."

"So you noticed her huge breasts, did you?" Monica asked.

"A blind person could've seen them."

"Lucky for you, you have 20-20 vision," Monica snapped. She yanked his shirt over her head and tossed it on the bed.

"What the hell are you doing?"

"I'm leaving." She grabbed the clothes she had tossed on the chair by the dresser and started getting dressed.

"You can't be serious."

"What would you do if you found another man's drawers in my bed?" He didn't answer. "Exactly. You'd be upset and demand answers, and if I gave the weak, pathetic answers you gave me, you'd agree they were unsatisfactory too."

"Godammit, Monica, you know I didn't have another woman in here. I wouldn't cheat on you."

"I don't know shit. I know what I see, and what I see is not good."

"You're looking for an excuse to run because I told you that I love you."

"Oh sure, that's it. Not because we found another woman's panties in your bed. That couldn't be it at all," she said snidely.

"You're not leaving." Andre snatched her blouse.

Monica snatched it back. "You can't keep me here." She

dragged the top over her head, picked up her handbag, and bolted for the sliding door.

Andre grabbed her arm. "Monica."

She pulled away. "Let me go!" Tears filled her eyes. "I don't know what to think right now. I need time to *think*." She shook with emotion. This wasn't supposed to happen. Everything was perfect. Why was their relationship falling apart again?

"I love you." His eyes begged her to believe him.

Monica squeezed her eyes shut. "That's what you say, but how do I know I can trust you? I want to believe you, but I'm not going to be your fool, Andre."

"I'm telling you, it was Daisy. You haven't noticed she dresses like you? She did all of that to get my attention. *This*." He pointed at the thong behind him on the bed. "This was the final step to break us apart."

Monica did notice Daisy's entire style had changed, but she'd seen it as a positive, which meant she had been a good influence on her assistant.

Information overload gave her a headache. She rubbed her temples. She needed time away from Andre.

"I need to go." She opened the door and rushed toward the staircase.

He didn't stop her again, and she wasn't sure if she was relieved or if that hurt more.

Inside her SUV, she took a moment to calm the shaking in her hands. This was Andre. Maybe Daisy did try to sabotage them, but why? To steal Andre away from Monica? She had never seen any indication Daisy was interested in him, but maybe she didn't notice because she hadn't been paying attention.

She needed to know for sure before making a hasty decision. The expression on Andre's face haunted her. Surprise.

Disappointment. Surely he could understand why she needed to be certain.

Driving out of the parking lot, she dialed Daisy's number.

"Hello?" Her assistant sounded groggy.

Monica didn't care if she woke her up. She needed answers more than she cared about Daisy getting enough sleep.

"I need you to meet me at the house."

"Now?"

"Yes, now. It's important."

Pause.

"Okay, I'll be there."

Monica never expected a different answer. Whenever she called, Daisy made herself available. On the long drive home, she tortured herself with negative thoughts. Could the underwear belong to Belinda? Were they back together, or did he meet a new woman who captured his attention?

Stop! she screamed inside her head. Answers first, speculation later.

At home, she parked her car and raced up to her room, still wired from the conversation with Andre. If their roles had been reversed, he would be upset.

More than anything, she needed to talk to Daisy face to face. At the moment, Daisy was a trusted confidante, and she needed to see her face when she questioned her. She didn't want what Andre said to be true, but if what he said wasn't true, then he had lied to her.

Either way, betrayal would come from someone in her life who she cared deeply about.

Her phone chimed. A text from Andre. Three words.

You know me.

Monica swallowed the lump in her throat.

Daisy entered the room, her footsteps hesitant. "Hi. What's going on?"

"Have a seat," Monica said.

Daisy sat on the edge of the bed and cupped her hands together like a little kid awaiting a scolding. "It's been a while. It's good to see you."

"You might not feel that way after we get through with this conversation."

Monica figured the easiest way to get through this conversation and to the heart of the matter, was to be blunt.

"I went over to Andre's tonight, and we found a pair of panties in his bed that don't belong to me. Did you put them there?"

Daisy's mouth fell open. "How or why would I do something so awful?"

"That's what I want to know. He said you came over there about a flat tire, and at some point you went into the apartment."

"To use the bathroom."

"You didn't plant a purple thong in his bed?"

"Oh my goodness, absolutely not! Did he accuse me of putting them there?"

Monica examined her. She seemed genuinely perturbed. "If you didn't plant the underwear..." She didn't want to think of the alternative, which meant they belonged to someone else.

Daisy lowered her eyes. "This is so awkward. I know how much you care about him, so I didn't want to say anything..."

Monica's heart beat against her ribs. "If you have something to say, say it."

Daisy bit her bottom lip. "I don't want to hurt you. You're more than my employer, you're my friend."

"I also see you as a friend. What do you have to tell me?" Her chest tightened under the strain of needing to know.

"Andre... he acted strange when I picked up your dress while you were in Miami, I brushed it off. I probably shouldn't have stopped at his apartment tonight, but I needed help. I didn't know how to change a tire, and I got a flat. I feel... I feel like this is my fault."

Fear seized Monica's heart. "What are you talking about? Wh-what's your fault?"

Daisy swallowed. "While I was there, Andre made a pass at me."

"He did what?" Her worst fear. It couldn't be true.

"I'm so sorry, Monica. I didn't want to tell you, but since he's accusing me of planting panties in the bed—well, I can't let him get away with it."

Monica backed away. "I don't believe you."

"Believe me, I was as shocked as you are. After he changed the tire, I was ready to go, but he asked if I wanted to come inside for a second. I hesitated but didn't want to be rude because he had helped me out, so I said okay. When I went inside, he asked if I wanted something to drink, and I said no, I should be on my way. That didn't stop him. He poured us each a glass of wine and made comments about how much you and I look alike. Honestly, he made me uncomfortable. When he took off his shirt—"

"He took off his shirt!" Monica exclaimed.

Daisy nodded, seeming to shrink into her body. "When he tried to kiss me, I ran out of there as fast as I could."

Monica felt as if someone was strangling her with a thick rope. "Why would he do that? It doesn't make sense." Her mind clawed in desperation at an alternative explanation.

"His behavior didn't make sense to me either, but I think the similarities between us caused him to... I don't know."

Monica kept her eyes on Daisy. She didn't seem to be lying. "You said he took off his shirt?"

"Yes."

"What's the tattoo on his chest?" If she couldn't answer the question, Monica would know she was lying.

"A trail of stars. He said he got them because of his Grandpa Cy."

The floor beneath Monica's feet tilted sideways, and she staggered to the wall to avoid collapsing.

Daisy rushed over and placed a hand on her shoulder. "Monica, I'm sorry. I would have taken what happened last night to my grave. I hope you can forgive me for telling."

Monica's mouth remained stuck in an open position, and pain ripped through her. She was being torn in half, the damning words ripping asunder any dreams of a future with Andre. "I... I was ready to tell him that I loved him." Her lower lip trembled.

"He doesn't deserve your love. He tried to seduce me, so he's probably done the same with other women. That would explain the panties."

Monica burst into tears, and Daisy wrapped comforting arms around her. "It's going to be okay. I'm here, and you can trust me. I'll make sure you're okay."

Monica sobbed into her shoulder, and eventually Daisy helped her into bed. Monica curled up on her side and closed her eyes tight. Tears seeped past her lids onto the pillow.

"Do you need anything?" Daisy asked in a gentle voice.

"No." She could barely talk. She sniffled.

"I'm not leaving, okay? I told you I will always be here for you, and that hasn't changed. Get some rest. You've been through a lot in one night." She patted Monica's arm.

Monica pulled the covers over her head and sobbed into the pillow.

Eventually she fell asleep, exhausted, with Daisy right by her side.

Chapter Thirty-Two

Monica woke up slowly. Her swollen eyes creaked open, and she sensed the lateness of the morning though the blackout drapes kept sunlight from pouring into the room.

Daisy typed away on the computer on the table by the window.

"Good morning," Monica croaked, voice hoarse from crying.

"Hey, you're awake." A bright smile lit up her assistant's face.

Monica stared at her in disbelief. "You cut off all your hair."

"I did," Daisy said, smoothing her hair from the crown to her nape. "I wanted to surprise you. I left early this morning and went to a barbershop. I showed the barber a picture of you from IG, told him I wanted your cut, and he went to work. What do you think? Now we'll really be twins!"

What the hell? Unease leached into Monica's bones.

"I, um... it looks fine," she said.

"You don't like it." Daisy sounded devastated.

"No, it's just... I really liked your pixie cut, and I'm... surprised, that's all." She sat up in the bed and rubbed remnants of sleep from her eyes. "What time is it?"

"Almost ten-thirty."

"Wow, it's late. Did you stay the whole night?"

Daisy nodded. "I didn't want to leave in case you needed me."

"You didn't have to do that." Monica felt guilty about her negative thought moments ago. Daisy was a good friend, and she didn't deserve her. So what if she'd copied Monica's hairstyle? Sure it was a little strange, but it wasn't so unusual for friends to have stylistic similarities, right?

"What kind of friend would I be if I bailed when you needed me? Now, what would you like for breakfast?" Daisy closed the laptop and stood.

"I don't think I can eat."

Her entire being felt empty and more than anything, her heart ached. She was still in disbelief about Andre. She didn't need food. She needed time away. A trip would help—a stay in one of her family member's homes in another part of the country or overseas.

"You have to try. How about something simple, like toast and eggs? Fruit and yogurt?"

Monica swung her legs over the side of the bed and sat without moving. Did last night really happen? "I'll take fruit and coffee."

"Sounds good." Daisy came over and gave her a hug. "It'll get easier. I promise."

"I know," she said dully.

It did before, the last time she and Andre broke up. Getting rid of the pain would take time, but eventually she would return to her old self.

"Where's my phone?" She tossed a glance around the room.

"I have it. Andre texted you late last night, and I didn't want him to disturb your rest."

Her foolish heart jumpstarted despite knowing he couldn't be trusted. "What did he say?"

"He wanted to talk and blamed me again, but I responded as you and told him you wanted to be left alone. I hope that was okay."

True enough, Daisy had responded to texts on her behalf before, but this was different. It was personal.

"In the future, I can handle communications with Andre. I want my phone now." She put out her hand.

"No problem." Daisy went to the table and brought back the phone. "I deleted the messages because I didn't want them to upset you. As a friend, I think it's best for you to not have any contact with him. We can have someone pick up your clothes and other belongings at his place, so neither of us have to see him."

Monica nodded. "Good idea."

"I'll make the arrangements when I return from getting your breakfast. I'll be back soon."

After she left, Monica sat on the bed, numb. How could Andre have done this to her, after everything they had shared over the past couple months? The day after she introduced him to her family! He not only cheated, he tried to seduce her assistant. She didn't know him at all.

Her face crumbled. Fisting her hands, she fought the urge to burst into tears. No more. He didn't deserve more of her tears.

She dragged to the bathroom, brushed her teeth, and went through her facial cleansing routine. Rubbing moisturizer into her skin, she replayed the conversation with Daisy from last night.

Frowning, she cocked her head to the side. Her brain snagged on a detail that didn't make sense. Slowly, she replaced the jar of moisturizer on the counter.

Heart racing, she went over the conversation again. She had been so distraught and caught up in emotion, she overlooked an important point in the story.

Daisy had lied.

Hearing movement in the bedroom, Monica rushed out the bathroom, ready to confront Daisy. She was placing a tray of food on the table by the window.

"Rodolfo and I agreed fruit would not be enough. In addition to a fruit salad, he prepared scrambled eggs and toast in case you had enough appetite to eat a little more."

"Thanks." Monica switched gears. A direct confrontation wouldn't be best. She cleared her throat. "Um, could you tell me the story again, of what Andre did after he invited you into his apartment?"

"Why?"

"I want you to tell me again." Monica hoped her voice didn't sound accusatory, though a anger threatened to derail her calm.

"Like I said, he invited me inside, and I went against my better judgment."

"Mhmm. Then what happened?"

"He asked if I wanted something to drink, and I turned him down, but he insisted. He poured two glasses of wine, which I thought was odd, because I thought he was offering water or juice when he asked if I wanted something to drink."

"Why do you think he chose wine?"

"To set the mood. Maybe to get me tipsy? I can't begin to rationalize the behavior of someone like him."

No change in her speech. No discernible signs of dishonesty.

"Did you drink any of the wine? Did he?"

"I took a sip. He drank most of his while we talked."

"Interesting, because Andre doesn't drink wine," Monica said.

Tomb-like silence engulfed the room. Heart racing like a jackrabbit, Monica waited for Daisy to respond.

"H-he doesn't?"

"No."

"He did last night."

"No, he didn't. I haven't seen him drink wine the entire time he and I have been back together. When we're together, if I drink wine, he drinks rum and coke or vodka or something else. You lied to me."

"No, I didn't."

Monica saw the cracks in her armor, panic blanketing her face.

"How do you explain how I know what his chest looks like?" Daisy demanded.

"I don't have an explanation. You tell me how you happened to see his chest."

"Monica—"

"You lied to me!" Monica yelled.

Daisy jumped and fear stretched her eyes wide.

"Was your plan to go after him next? Did you think he would want you after he and I broke up?"

Daisy didn't respond, but the tears brimming her eyes spoke volumes.

"Answer me!" Monica screamed.

"I didn't do it for him. I did it for you," Daisy whispered in a trembling voice.

"What do you mean you did it for me?"

"He was coming between us. We're best friends. You spend all your time over there now, and I never see you. You cut me out. We don't go on smoothie runs anymore, and our weekly meetings no longer exist because all of sudden you think it's fine for us to work virtually through phone calls and emails. You took him to Bruno's party, and you didn't invite *me*."

Monica stared at Daisy in disbelief. "You're jealous of Andre?"

Daisy hung her head and angrily wiped away the tears scrolling down her cheeks.

"Oh my goodness."

She scrutinized her assistant with a new set of eyes. The shaved head, the new clothes, the lost weight. She had turned herself into a clone of Monica. Not because she wanted Andre, but because she was obsessed and wanted to *be* Monica.

She reflected on all the times they had spent together, Daisy's comments about wanting the same type of car, the switch to regularly drinking smoothies and preferring the same ones Monica did.

She didn't know if to feel anger or pity.

"You're fired. You need to go," Monica said.

Daisy's head snapped up, and her eyes widened in dismay. "No! Monica, please don't shut me out. I promise, I won't do anything like that again."

"So you admit you planted the panties and lied about Andre making a pass at you."

"Y-yes, but I-I didn't know what else to do. You were ignoring me. Friends don't treat friends like that."

Monica swallowed, her belly twisting into a thousand knots of dread. Years ago, Ignacio had the unfortunate experience of being stalked by a woman who swore he was her one true love and declared him the father of her unborn child. He secured a restraining order and didn't think much about the woman until he came home one day and found her waiting in his bed. He said he was not only alarmed, it was the creepiest sensation in the world to have an obsessed fan inside his home.

Monica now understood a bit of what he went through. She experienced the same creepy sensation, made worse because she and Daisy had been friends. Daisy had access to her emails, her home, her family, her life, which made her behavior even more disturbing.

"You can't cut me off," Daisy wailed, her face crumbling.

Monica edged toward the door. "I-I could never trust you again."

Daisy followed and slammed her palms to her chest. "I give you my word, I will never do anything like this again. I realize the mistake I made, and I'm sorry. I didn't mean to hurt you. You're my idol. I love you."

She reached for Monica, but Monica dodged her and ran out the door.

"Monica, wait. I'm not going to hurt you. I—"

Monica dashed down the stairs. "Rodolfo, help! Rodolfo!" she yelled.

By the time she reached the bottom of the stairs, the chef was already there. "Monica, what's wrong?"

She ran behind him and gazed up at Daisy, who halted halfway down the staircase.

"She needs to leave," Monica said. Her heart thumped hard against her chest.

Daisy sank onto the stairs and covered her face. Sobbing into her hands. "I'm sorry."

She repeated the words over and over again.

Chapter Thirty-Three

After Rodolfo took on the role of security and escorted Daisy from the house, Monica called her attorney, Penelope, and alerted her to the situation with Daisy.

Penelope was apologetic, but Monica couldn't really blame her. They had done the appropriate background check, and the truth of the matter was, Daisy fooled them both.

Next, she locked Daisy out of all her systems. Working with her business manager, they change the passwords on the slush fund account she transferred money into every month for miscellaneous expenses, which Daisy had access to through a debit card. She also canceled the card.

They changed the passwords to the social media accounts and scrubbed Daisy's name from anywhere she had access to Monica's accounts.

The actions took hours, but by early afternoon, Monica's mind was at ease. Her family immediately offered a multitude of suggestions. Although she usually hated their overprotectiveness, she appreciated the concern this time and took all the advice they gave about being cautious, including the need for a temporary bodyguard. Daisy had not been violent but left the property as a devastated, broken down soul. She didn't want to take any changes.

Next, she planned to go see Andre but needed to prepare. She scoured her closet for the perfect outfit—one that would blow him away and convince him to accept her apology without hesitation. He liked her legs, so she chose an orange mini-dress with a flared skirt and halter top that left her back exposed. After one last turn in the closet's full-length mirror, she slipped on a pair of her favorite Mignonne heels and headed out the door.

She booked a last-minute spa appointment and got an all over body scrub and a cucumber treatment which did wonders for her puffy eyes. She felt like a new woman when she exited the back, but as she walked into the open waiting room, she pulled up short, and her heart hammered to a stop in her chest.

Andre sat two seats down from her driver-bodyguard. He wore a fitted tee—which laid bare his tattoos—and worn out jeans, but might as well have been wearing a tailored designer suit. He looked scrumptious, and she ached to fling herself into his arms.

"Hi," she whispered.

What a lame greeting. She wished she could think of something more impactful to say, but all the words she had rehearsed scattered, like dust, from her brain.

He stood, face stony, jaw line firm. "I went by the house, and your mother told me where to find you and your bodyguard. Tell him to go." He angled his head toward the burly blond. "You're coming with me. I'll make sure you're safe."

The bodyguard rose slowly to his feet, keeping his eyes on Andre. "Ma'am, do you need me to handle this?"

"No, there's no need for handling anything," Monique said quickly. "You can leave."

"You're sure, ma'am?"

"Positive. Please take my car to the house."

After a moment's hesitation, the man nodded and left the premises.

Andre continued to glower at her. Monica knew he'd be upset, nonetheless her heart sank. Winning him over was going to be hard. She approached him on unsteady feet, belly a tangled weave of trepidation.

He spun away from her and held open the door. Monica slipped past, racking her brain for something to say to break the icy chill exuding from him. She came up short.

Once they settled in the Escalade, she turned to him. "Andre, I—"

"Not now. We'll talk at the apartment." He didn't look at her.

She slumped in the seat.

Finally, they arrived at the apartment and entered. Andre tossed his keys on the kitchen bar and faced her.

"So we're done," he said.

Was that a question or a statement? Monica couldn't be sure, but she tensed as panic seized her. "We argued. That doesn't mean we're broken up," she said, though she'd been prepared to end the relationship because she thought he cheated.

"Oh, we're changing the rules now? That's not what you said last night when you texted me."

Oh crap. "What did I text you?"

"You're playing dumb?"

"I'm not playing dumb. I honestly don't know what you

received in the text. Daisy responded as me. All I know is, she told you I wanted to be alone."

"The return text said a lot more than that. It told me to go fuck myself, called me a liar, and said you never wanted to hear from me again because we were done. Are you saying that's not how you felt last night after you ran out of here, believing I had brought another woman to my apartment and slept with her in the same bed you and I share?" He walked slowly over to her, anger rolling off him.

Normally when she wore heels, they stood almost eye to eye, but his body seemed to have widened, and she could almost swear he had grown at least three inches. Fury tightened his skin, making the bones in his face more prominent and the scar in his eyebrow paler.

"I–I admit I was upset," Monica stammered. "But I never wrote that text to you."

He communicated his displeasure with glaring eyes.

Her body quaked. She didn't like this version of Andre. She wanted the one who adored her, paid her compliments, and smiled whenever she appeared.

"I was going to come to you. I know Daisy lied."

"Oh, you know. Please, tell me how you figured that out?" He crossed his arms over his chest and waited.

Taking a deep breath, Monica repeated the story Daisy told her. While she recounted the tale of him supposedly inviting her inside, Andre didn't react. The only physical response was a deeper frown when she recounted how Daisy claimed she fled after he tried to kiss her.

"That's quite a story."

"I didn't want to believe her, but I had to protect my heart. I remembered being crushed when you dumped me in college. Then this morning I realized what she said couldn't be right.

You don't drink wine. If she lied about that, the rest of the story lacked credibility."

"I definitely didn't take off my shirt to seduce her. When she came by to pick up your dress, I had my shirt off because I'd finished exercising not too long before she arrived."

"I figured that part of the story was a lie."

"I see. So if she hadn't made the mistake of saying I drank wine, you would have continued to believe *I* lied. Right?"

"I would have eventually figured out the truth," Monica said in a small voice.

He scrutinized her with narrowed eyes. "You know what I realize? You don't trust me. After all this time and everything I've done, the past few months we've spent together don't mean anything to you."

"That's not true. I made a mistake, and I'm sorry. It's not that I don't trust you. I just wasn't sure."

"I don't know how else to prove that I care about you. To prove how much you mean to me."

"Don't," Monica pleaded. "I believe you care about me."

"Now you do. What happens in a few months when something else crops up?"

"Nothing else will crop up. This is it. I'm good," she promised.

"You're good, but I'm not. Maybe *I* need to think."

Her heart sank. "About what?"

"About whether or not our relationship is going to work. Seems pretty fucking fragile."

"Andre, there was a random thong in your bed. You can't blame me for being suspicious."

"No, but when I told you about Daisy, you should have listened."

"I did listen, which is why I confronted her, but she created a story that made me have doubts."

"Yeah, well, now I have doubts. I don't know why I came to get you."

"Because we belong together," Monica whispered. She was wearing her heart on her sleeve. Couldn't he see? "You have to forgive me. I'm not leaving until you forgive me. I don't care if it takes days. You're going to have to put me out, and when you do, I-I'll use my key and come right back in."

He continued to look at her as if she was crazy. "What exactly are you fighting for?" he asked.

The answer was simple. There was no other answer to give. "Us."

One word. Two letters. The embodiment of their relationship and everything they meant to each other.

Monica showed him the tattoo on the inside of her wrist. "We're always going to be together." Emotion made her voice tremble.

"You can't even tell me that you love me," Andre said, his voice raw and gravelly.

Monica took the few short steps to reach him. "You said you knew," she whispered.

He swallowed. "Maybe I need to hear it."

She looked deeply into his eyes, not wanting to leave any doubt about her feelings. "I love you, Andre. *I love you.*"

She smiled. Simply by admitting her love for him, a weight had been lifted from her shoulders.

"I'll say it every day if you want me to."

She heard Andre's labored breaths as he stared her. She waited for his next move but meant every word she said. She would not leave until he forgave her.

He took one step closer and roughly dragged her into his arms. With a sigh of relief, Monica dived into the searing, soul-wrenching kiss that ensued.

One hand went to the back of her neck, and his fingers circled and tightened. Andre grabbed her in a way that screamed that she belonged to him.

No, they belonged to each other.

Chapter Thirty-Four

His kisses were like candy, flavorful and addictive. Andre plundered her mouth and both of them groaned as they were sucked into a swirling vortex of desire. He shoved Monica against the wall, his hard body pinning her while one knee slid between her thighs and pried them apart.

His turgid length pressed into her belly, a sweet promise that made her cling to him and lift one leg to his waist while she stretched onto her toes so their hips lined up perfectly. He pressed harder into her, grinding into her heated, achy core. Squeezing her breast, his thumb flicked across the tight nipple, and she shuddered. Scorching pleasure tore through her blood and made her knees tremble.

Panting hard, she undid his belt and then his zipper with frantic hands and shoved the jeans past his hips. His magnificent, beautiful, hard dick stood at attention, the engorged head already moistened with precum—so tempting she couldn't decide which hole she wanted it in.

Andre wrested the decision from her when he tore off her

thong with an impatient tug. He kicked one leg out of his jeans and hoisted her against the wall. She lifted the hem of her dress higher so it bunched around her waist and ground her moist clef against his shaft.

She kissed his shoulders and neck. She caressed his face, her eyes worshiping his handsome, rough-hewn features.

"There's no one else in the world for me," she whispered. "I love you, Andre."

"I love you, Andre," she whispered. "There's no one else in the world for me."

He thrust into her with an agonized groan.

His hands gripped her slim hips, and her arms tightened around his strong neck. He sliced into her with a rapid motion, and their mouths crashed together again with heated pants colliding against each other's lips.

Each time their hips smacked together, she whimpered. No one else made her feel like this. He took complete control of her body. She was his to use at will.

With steady, fierce strokes, Andre took her higher and higher to a mind-numbing peak. She licked the sweat that popped out on his neck and flung her head back, overcome with pleasure. He sucked on her arched throat and squeezed her ass.

"You feel so goddamn good. I could stay inside you. All. Day. And. Night." He spoke through gritted teeth, punctuating his words with pelvic thrusts.

She came hard, trembling in his arms and spasming around him. At the same time, he dropped his head to her shoulder, grinding his hips into hers as he groaned through his own powerful climax.

Monica clung to him, burying her face in his neck. Tears of relief flooded her eyes.

Thank goodness he'd forgiven her.

* * *

Stretching like a satisfied cat, Monica rolled onto her stomach and watched Andre with her chin propped on her hand.

Feeling pretty satisfied himself, he reclined against the pillows with one arm folded behind his head. When he received the text last night stating they were finished, he had been devastated. Then he brooded over the callous and ridiculous nature of breaking up by text, particularly since he never got a chance to truly talk to her about the situation. Eventually, his pain turned to anger, which prompted him to track her down and demand an explanation.

"What are you thinking?" she asked.

"How much I missed you during that short period." He stroked her cheek with the back of his hand.

"I'm glad you're not mad at me anymore," she said.

"Who says I'm not mad at you?"

"You can't stay mad at me."

No, he couldn't. Monica had full control of his heart.

"So I'm guessing you fired Daisy?"

"I did. You don't know the half of what happened."

She summarized the morning's events, which left him shocked.

"She was interested in you?"

"Not in a sexual way—more an obsessive fan way."

"Are you all right?"

"She didn't hurt me."

"But it's traumatic, to know she was trying to sabotage your life to keep you to herself."

"Yeah, it's very Single White Female-ish, but in Black." Monica shivered.

"I'm glad you have a sense of humor."

She fell silent for a moment. "I don't think she meant me

any harm. I actually feel sorry for her. I think she's lonely, and I was probably her only friend."

"Maybe. I'm glad you got away from her, though. You never know how bad her obsession could become."

"I have an inkling. One time, a fan stalked Ignacio for months. She ended up breaking into his house and climbed into his bed. It freaked him out."

"I bet it did. You need to be careful, Monica. You share a lot of your life online and sometimes give out your location."

"Don't worry, I'll be careful. That's why I hired the bodyguard, at least for now, until we're certain Daisy doesn't mean any harm."

"Good." Andre breathed a little easier and allowed a smile to break out on his face. "I have something for you. I was supposed to give it to you this morning, but you showed your ass last night."

"You're never going to let me live this down, are you?"

"No."

"I love you," she said sweetly.

"Uh-huh."

He gave her quick smack on the lips and slipped naked from the bed.

"What is it?" she asked, excitement in her voice. Monica enjoyed receiving gifts. She sat up.

"It's a surprise."

Andre went into the closet and pulled a small rose gold pouch with a drawstring from a box on the top shelf. Hiding the gift behind his back, he approached the bed.

"Close your eyes and put out your hand."

She grinned, closing her eyes and extending both hands.

"One hand. It's not that big."

She giggled. "Okay." She held out her right hand.

Andre placed the little bag in the middle of her palm and sat on the side of the bed. "Open your eyes."

She stared at the bag. "What's this?"

"Open it."

"Did I forget an anniversary or something?" she asked, sounding genuinely concerned.

"No. Now open the bag so you can actually see what's inside and stop worrying."

She did and gasped when she upended the contents into her palm. A pair of diamond earrings glittered against her skin. The round design displayed a main diamond surrounded by an impressive halo of pavé-set diamond accents.

"You remember these?" Andre asked in a low, husky voice.

Monica lifted her gaze to his. "Of course I remember. I can't believe you kept them."

He couldn't believe he kept them either. He could have easily pawned or sold the earrings to recoup some of his cost, but neither option seemed right. The only right decision had been to hold onto them indefinitely. He gave them to her for their one year anniversary back in college, the same night they got the tattoos. He saved for months, and having her wear them had filled him with a sense of pride.

When they broke up and she tossed them at him with angry tears, he had been gutted. Since he no longer had the box they'd come in, he purchased the drawstring bag to keep them safe.

"Put them in," he said.

Monica removed the earrings she currently wore and replaced them with the diamonds. Perfection. They brought her eyes to life and sparkled against her russet-brown skin.

Angling her head sideways, she showed off her profile. "How do I look?"

"Beautiful. Sexy. Like a million bucks."

"I love them more than the first day you gave them to me. Thank you." She looped her arms around his neck and kissed him hard, her soft lips and tongue an erotic tease.

His body stirred again, and he eased her onto her back. "Nobody comes between us again. Not your mother, your stepfather, your friends, my family, my friends—nobody. Got it?"

"Got it. Say you love me," she said.

Andre locked both of her hands above her head. "I love you. I'll love you forever."

She gazed at him with adoration in her eyes, the kind of look that made men start wars and bar brawls.

"Forever with you ain't enough, Andre Campos."

"For me either. I guess we'll have to make do," he whispered.

Then he kissed her and slid between her thighs for another round.

Chapter Thirty-Five

Andre pulled the Escalade beside the speaker at the drive-thru. Leaning out the window, he placed an order for a chocolate smoothie and a green smoothie enhanced with muscle builder.

After he collected the beverages, he handed Monica her chocolate smoothie and took a sip of his. "Not bad."

"Told you. Park over there. I want to take a picture." She propped her bare feet on the dashboard, and the hem of her sundress slid down her thighs.

"Tease." Andre kissed the side of her knee and dragged his warm hand along the inside of her thigh, exposing more flesh for his hungry eyes.

His touch heated her skin and made her body tingle, but Monica pried his hand off her thigh. "Behave. I'm trying to get a shot."

"You and your perfect shots."

"One of these days I'm going to convince you to let me post your photo."

"Never."

"We'll see."

She fixed her dress and held the smoothie at arms-length, making sure to capture her feet propped on the dashboard. She didn't like the shot, so she tried again. After three more attempts, a request to move the vehicle to a different location to make better use of the sun, and audible, exasperated sighs coming from Andre, she finally captured the carefree image she wanted to post.

"You can go now," she said, sweetly.

"Thank you," Andre muttered.

She ignored him and typed a quick caption: *My current situation.*

They were on their way to the location of his future lounge. Ethan deposited the money into Andre's account two weeks ago, and the workers started today. When they pulled into the gravel lot, he parked a safe distance away from the warehouse.

Men in safety goggles and hard hats moved in and out of the building. Scaffolding climbed the front, and two dumpsters —one already full—collected trash, debris, and unusable parts of the interior the men tore out.

She and Andre climbed out of the vehicle and observed the work from in front of the Escalade. Andre's dream was about to come true, and she couldn't be prouder.

"I'm going live. You want to be in the shot?"

"What do you think?"

She rolled her eyes but respected his decision.

Standing with her back to the construction site, she held up the camera, making sure to capture her best angle and the work behind her. She went live, flashing a smile to her followers.

"I'm not telling you what this is, but it's going to be *huge.* All caps," she said in a conspiratorial tone. "You know I always

have the scoop. More details coming soon. Tah-tah, bitches."
She smirked and blew a kiss at the camera. Then she ended the
video.

"Huge, all caps?" Andre said.

Monica shrugged. "Everything about you is huge."

He pulled her close, molding her to his body. "You sure
know how to stroke a man's ego."

"It's the truth," she cooed.

They kissed, and he slipped his tongue into her mouth.

"Mmm." Monica caressed the muscles of his corded arms
and hunched his thigh.

"Damn. You better behave before I screw you in front of all
these men."

His hand slipped to her backside and squeezed, and she
made a whimpering sound to let him know how much she
liked it.

His phone rang and they both groaned, annoyed.

"Hello?"

Monica stepped away so he could talk.

"This is he."

Afterward, all she heard was mhmm, two okays, and a
when, but as soon as he hung up, Andre doubled over and
buried his face in his hands.

"Baby?" Monica placed a hand on his back. what could
be wrong? She immediately went into protective mode.
When he straightened, she grabbed his face. "What
happened?"

"Nothing. Everything is perfect."

His face transformed into a smile wider than any she had
ever seen on his face.

"That was my mother's attorney. They got my mom
another trial," he said in a thick voice.

Monica screamed and flung her arms around his neck. She

gave him a big kiss. "That's great news. I'm so happy, I can't believe it!"

"Best news I've ever had. I'ma do this. I'ma get her out." The confidence in his voice sparked a wave of joy in her heart.

"Yes, you are. I knew you could do it."

He blew out a long breath and let his head fall back to gaze up at the sky. "Thank you," he whispered.

They spent another half hour at the location. Before leaving, Andre spoke to the foreman for a few minutes and then they started the drive back to his apartment.

Monica walked in ahead of him, and once inside, he caught her hand and pulled her around to face him.

"You're the best thing that ever happened to me. Do you know that?"

Shaking her head, Monica melted into him and wrapped her arms around his waist.

His eyes turned intense as he cupped her cheek. "You are. After the lounge is up and running and I earn my degree, we're getting married. I want to feel this happy every day, and that'll only happen if I spend the rest of my life with you."

Emotion clogged her throat as she recalled the conversation with her Aunt Florence. Getting married no longer seemed outdated, and being tied to one man no longer terrified her. Losing Andre had been the problem all along. She had met and lost her one true love, and anyone else was only a substitute. Andre made her feel happy, safe, and loved.

"I only want to spend the rest of my life with *you*," Monica whispered.

His eyelids grew heavy with hunger, and he pulled her bottom lip between his teeth. "Now, about that screwing I mentioned back at the warehouse."

Andre swept her up in his arms, and Monica squealed her delight. Carrying her the way a groom would carry his bride across the threshold, Andre climbed the stairs and Monica locked her arms around his neck.

One day he would carry her across the threshold of their home after they said their vows.

She could hardly wait.

Also by Delaney Diamond

More from the Family Ties series!

Ethan (Family Ties #1)

After seven years together, one night, Skye Thorpe broaches the subject of marriage and learns the devastating truth. Ethan has no intention of marrying her.

Monica (Family Ties #2)

* * *

More family series are available!

Visit my Books page to learn about all my books and the

Johnson Family

Brooks Family

Hawthorne Family

* * *

Audiobook samples and free short stories available at www.delaneydiamond.com.

About the Author

Delaney Diamond is the USA Today Bestselling Author of sensual, passionate romance novels. Originally from the U.S. Virgin Islands, she now lives in Atlanta, Georgia. She reads romance novels, mysteries, thrillers, and a fair amount of nonfiction. When she's not busy reading or writing, she's in the kitchen trying out new recipes, dining at one of her favorite restaurants, or traveling to an interesting locale.

Enjoy free reads on her website. Join her mailing list to get sneak peeks, notices of sale prices, and find out about new releases.

Join her mailing list
www.delaneydiamond.com

facebook.com/DelaneyDiamond

twitter.com/DelaneyDiamond

bookbub.com/authors/delaney-diamond

pinterest.com/delaneydiamond

$\#14.99$

Made in the USA
Middletown, DE
29 October 2022